"What, No Comment?"

She shook her head.

"Strange," he went on, "I never thought that you would allow any man to have you without his ring on your finger!"

"I didn't think so, either," she said with a gasp.

He bent over her again. His mouth was hard and demanding against hers. He placed his hands on either side of her face. "I want you so very much," he whispered. "Do you want me?"

"Yes," she burst out.

He kissed her one last time. "Good," he said. "You can never ~~~~ ombón, always re~

ELIZABE

uses the w~ ~ts with
broad, col~ ~ ~ ~he is meticulous in
her eye for detail. Well known for her delightful characters, she is internationally loved by her loyal and enthusiastic readers.

Dear Reader:

I'd like to take this opportunity to thank you for all your support and encouragement of Silhouette Romances.

Many of you write in regularly, telling us what you like best about Silhouette, which authors are your favorites. This is a tremendous help to us as we strive to publish the best contemporary romances possible.

All the romances from Silhouette Books are for you, so enjoy this book and the many stories to come. I hope you'll continue to share your thoughts with us, and invite you to write to us at the address below:

Karen Solem
Editor-in-Chief
Silhouette Books
P.O. Box 769
New York, N.Y. 10019

ELIZABETH HUNTER
A Silver Nutmeg

Silhouette Romance

Published by Silhouette Books New York

America's Publisher of Contemporary Romance

For Lucien—of course!

SILHOUETTE BOOKS, a Simon & Schuster Division of
GULF & WESTERN CORPORATION
1230 Avenue of the Americas, New York, N.Y. 10020

Copyright © 1982 by Elizabeth Hunter

Distributed by Pocket Books

All rights reserved, including the right to reproduce
this book or portions thereof in any form whatsoever.
For information address Silhouette Books, 1230
Avenue of the Americas, New York, N.Y. 10020

ISBN: 0-671-57167-2

First Silhouette Books printing August, 1982

10 9 8 7 6 5 4 3 2 1

All of the characters in this book are fictitious. Any resemblance to actual persons, living or dead, is purely coincidental.

Map by Tony Ferrara

SILHOUETTE, SILHOUETTE ROMANCE and colophon
are registered trademarks of Simon & Schuster.

America's Publisher of Contemporary Romance

Printed in the U.S.A.

Other Silhouette Books by Elizabeth Hunter

The Lion's Shadow
Bride of the Sun
A Touch of Magic
Written in the Stars
One More Time

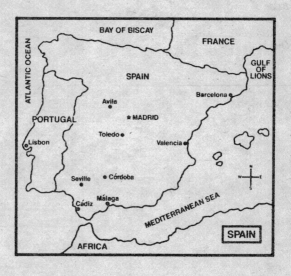

Chapter One

With a whole day to spare, Judi Duggan had taken herself to Avila. She was seated now at the small shrine of Cuatro Postes, looking across at the magnificent walled town of St. Teresa. The scene seemed strangely familiar to her, but then how many times had she seen these same walls in films. They had appeared in *El Cid*, and again in the dramatisation of C. S. Forrester's *The Gun*. It was hard to believe that these magnificent, imposing walls had been put in hand at the end of the eleventh century. They appeared to be perfect, almost as though they had risen from the rocky ground only yesterday.

The River Adaja trickled through the valley between her and the town, a group of grubby children scuffling their feet through the muddy waters at the edges. All except one child, she noticed, who was clean and neat, and whose interest in the proceedings seemed to be entirely organisational. Unsuitably dressed in rust-coloured velvet, the girl issued her instructions in a high-pitched yell worthy of a veteran fla-menco singer. Judi was amused to see the will-ingness with which the other children obeyed her, however, marching up the hill towards her perch on the Cuatro Postes and keeping step as best they could.

At that moment, the child looked up towards the shrine and saw Judi sitting there. Her whole expression changed as she came tearing up the stony slope, a delighted smile breaking across her face.

"Hudi! Hudi! What do you do here?" she de-manded.

Bewildered, Judi looked at her more carefully, remembering the little Spanish girl who had sat in her grandmother's shadow when Judi had been interviewed by that aristocratic lady in London. Was it possible that this could be the same child? And what had been her name?

That resolved itself in a breathless rush. "Hudi! It's me, Fabiola! You remember me now?"

Judi smiled, pleased to see her with her hair blowing in the wind and with her shoes and socks carried in one not very clean hand. In London the child had hardly said two words. She had sat beside her grandmother, her back as stiff as a poker, her eyes demurely resting on her knees. She had called Judi señorita then, as proud and as well-mannered as her obviously well-bred grandmother.

"I remember," Judi said. "And it's Judi, not Hudi. Think you can say that?"

The child dismissed the suggestion with a shrug. "I prefer Hudi. I have got used to calling you Hudi in my mind. Why do you call it Judi?"

"That's how we pronounce Js in English."

"But now you are in Spain," the child said unwaveringly. "Hudi is a very nice name, no?"

"It looks as if I shall have to get used to it," Judi resigned herself. "What are you doing in Avila?"

"We came to greet the Saint on my mother's anniversary. She was named for her. It's one of my names also."

Judi was about to ask her if she meant it was her mother's birthday, when a car drew up behind them and a man stepped out, a look of pure fury on his face.

"Fabiola!"

The child quivered. "Sí, Papa." She put a timid hand into Judi's and turned towards her father. "This is Señorita Hudi, Papa, who comes to arrange the new chapel. Señorita, my father Don Joaquin de Arnalte y Pizzaro."

"Hudi?" The man was every bit as arrogant and unbending as his mother had been. He was a handsome devil, though. Tall and spare, with a strongly moulded face and tired, drooping eyelids hiding dark eyes that Judi suspected missed nothing that went on around him.

"Judi Duggan," she corrected quietly.

She could have sworn that for an instant the man had been amused by his daughter's pronunciation of her name, but then she thought she had been mistaken as he glared at the little girl.

9

"And these children?" he asked her.

"They are my troops in the war against the Arabs," she explained. "We are winning the battle."

"Naturally," her father said dryly. "But girls don't lead soldiers into battle, little one."

"Joan of Arc did! Hudi may like doing embroidery, but I don't!" she added rebelliously.

"Hudi—Señorita Duggan—may teach you to like it."

"Never!"

Judi was amused by the man's slip of the tongue and by the angry way he had caught himself up. She looked at him with renewed interest, thinking she had never seen a better example of the male sex. Not even his formal clothes could disguise his well-developed muscles and the glow of health that emanated from his strong, lean body.

She was less amused, however, when he said something to his daughter in such rapid Spanish that she couldn't understand, and the light died in Fabiola's eyes to be replaced by a look of sheer misery.

"Why should Mama care?"

"She needs your prayers."

The child shook her head. "She prayed enough for herself, and the Saint is praying for her. Me, I can't pray all day. I prefer to conduct wars and gain glory for our family name."

"You'd be very good at it," Judi put in with a nervous laugh. "Your troops would follow you to hell and back!"

"Yes, they would," Fabiola agreed. "They don't mind that I'm a *girl!*"

Her father sighed. "I'm very glad you're a girl."

Fabiola frowned at him. "I'm not! Girls never have any fun. Look at Mama!"

"Your Mama was ill all the time you knew her. She had fun before that—"

"Before *me*, you mean. I don't want to have to have children and be ill and die! I don't want to be a girl!"

So the mother was dead. Judi clasped the child's hand in her own, tipping Fabiola's head back with a casual finger to meet her smile.

"Your grandmother is very much alive," she reminded her. "How many children did she have?"

"Ten."

"Then don't you think there must have been something else the matter with your mother? Your grandmother seems a very tough lady."

Fabiola giggled. "Yes, she is. Only you must never tell her so, Hudi. Ladies are never tough in Spain. Are they, Papa?"

"Never," he agreed solemnly.

Judi glanced at him, but the drooping eyelids effectively hid his thoughts from her. She allowed her eyes to run over the strong lines of his body with an interest she didn't normally display in strange men. Of course he was going to be her employer, she excused herself, so it was natural to want to know something about him.

"Well, Miss Duggan? Do you approve?"

She blushed scarlet, annoyed that he should have caught her in her appraisal of him. "There—there's a strong family resemblance

11

between you and your daughter," she managed. "And between you and your mother."

"We are a tough family?"

She took a deep breath. "Yes," she agreed.

"You think you can cope with us?"

"Yes," she said again. She wasn't at all sure that she could, but she saw no point in admitting as much to him. "Besides," she went on quickly, "I won't be seeing much of you, will I? Your mother said I would have my own suite of rooms and could come and go as I liked."

He raised his eyebrows and she was surprised to see that his dark eyes were dancing with laughter. "My mother would prefer that arrangement," he agreed softly. "As for the rest of the family—we shall see. Fabiola and I wouldn't want you to get lonely."

"I'm used to being on my own," Judi protested.

"Nobody is ever on his own in Spain," Fabiola said, rejecting the idea. "We like to have lots of people about all the time. Abuela told you that. You forget I was there all the time she was talking to you. She said you would be very welcome to join the family for meals."

Judi pulled down the corner of her mouth, remembering the tone in which the words had been uttered. "Doña Maria was very kind, but I got the impression she wasn't accustomed to having strangers in her home. We understood each other—"

Don Joaquin cut her off with an abrupt gesture. "My mother is rather old-fashioned in her ways, señorita. You'll know when she becomes your friend as well as your employer because you'll cease to be *La Inglesa* and will probably be Hudi to her, too."

"Not Miss Duggan?" Judi enquired lightly.

"*La Inglesa* is so much more imposing. It's the only name I've known you by until today. The English woman who comes to design the needlework for the new chapel. You are somewhat younger than I had pictured you from the description. I suppose you are properly qualified for the task?"

Judi bridled angrily, telling him in a few brief sentences all about the Royal School of Needlework where she had trained and worked for the last few years. "The English were famous for their needlework in Anglo-Saxon times," she added for good measure, "and we've been known for our skill ever since."

"So my mother tells me. I should have thought our Spanish nuns would be more apt for the task—"

"Why?" Judi asked him, quite willing to interrupt him in her annoyance. "Why should they do any better?"

"Our nuns have always been able to embroider beautifully, since time immemorial," he told her somewhat smugly.

"If that's all you require, señor, I may as well go back to England. Your mother said that, having rebuilt your family chapel, you wanted new vestments, everything, to be designed with your family in mind. Your Spanish nuns may carry out the work if you wish, but are they capable of designing altar cloths and hassocks, copes and white embroidery, so that they mesh and are a fitting memorial for those who died? That is the idea, isn't it, that those of your family who died in the Civil War should be properly remembered?"

"The old chapel was destroyed," Fabiola put in excitedly. "A cannon was fired at it and there was a fire! It was fortunate the rest of the castle still stands. It was a lucky shot, wasn't it, Papa?"

"People died in that fire," her father answered her.

"Not very many. If I'd been there, I'd have rushed out and fired guns back at them and killed them all! I'd have made them rebuild the chapel too, not left it as a ruin for years and years. Mama would have liked a chapel of her own."

Don Joaquin merely looked bleak. "I hadn't realised so much was involved in furnishing a small family chapel," he admitted to Judi with a wry smile. "It was my wife's dearest wish, however, that the chapel should be restored and made beautiful again. If you can do that, Miss Duggan, I shall be in your debt no matter how much it costs me."

Judi looked back at him, feeling sorry for him. Not that he would relish her pity, she thought. He was too proud by half, proud of his family and proud of himself as a man, to see himself in need of female sympathy.

"I can do that," she said.

"Then you had better come home with us now," Don Joaquin suggested. "Avila is a long way from the *alcázar*."

"I'm not expected until tomorrow," Judi told him uncertainly.

He considered her for a long moment in silence. "What brought you to Avila, señorita?"

"The Saint brought her!" Fabiola insisted, astonished that he should ask.

"Is that true?"

"Well, yes," Judi admitted.

"You have a devotion for Saint Teresa?"

"I've read her books," Judi explained reluctantly. "Is there any reason why I shouldn't admire her?"

"None at all. So *La Inglesa* has a mystical turn of mind?"

"Like Mama!" Fabiola put in.

"Not really," Judi said, embarrassed. "I'm a very practical sort of person—not that Saint Teresa wasn't, in her way—but I'm not at all emotional. I've never allowed my heart to rule my head, and I never will."

"Very wise," Don Joaquin remarked. "Will we find your luggage at the hotel?"

"The Reina Isabella," Judi confirmed. "I was wondering whether to go to Madrid tonight because I didn't know how long it would take me to get to your castle in the morning. If it won't put you out, I'd really much rather go with you tonight."

Don Joaquin glanced down at his excited daughter. "Fabiola would prefer it, too," was all he said. Apparently he had no preferences at all as to what Judi did.

"They are very special sweets, Hudi," Fabiola explained on the ride back to Avila. "Papa gave me the money to get them for you. But you must eat them, most of them, because I've already eaten a great many."

Judi accepted the treat, taking a long time to examine the pretty box in which the sweets were packed, topped by a photograph of the walls of Avila lit up against the black of the night sky. Fabiola could scarcely contain herself, longing to help open the box and get at the sweets inside.

Judi took pity on her, biting into one of the sugar-and-beaten-egg trifles and getting some of the yellow centre on her chin. She found the excessive sweetness cloying and handed the rest of the box to Fabiola.

"Have one yourself?" she offered.

Fabiola looked doubtful. "May I, Papa?"

"Will you have one, señor?" Judi asked him hastily.

"I never eat sweets," he answered his eyes on the road ahead. His tone suggested all such things were strictly the delight of the female sex and the female sex alone.

"Too sweet for me," Judi agreed. "Fabiola will have to eat them all herself."

"As long as she isn't sick."

"I'm never sick!" Fabiola claimed.

Judi hoped she was right. She had an idea that if the child were to be sick her father would have very little sympathy for her. He looked as though he'd have very little sympathy for any weakness, especially female weakness. He wasn't her idea of a pleasant man, or even a nice one. His expression was stern, full of the unbending pride that she was sure was his major characteristic. He seldom smiled—at least he had not smiled much at her.

So why did he interest her almost to the exclusion of the rest of her surroundings. She had been thrilled to see something of Spain only that morning, and now she scarcely had time to view the passing scenery outside the car, so intent was she on exploring her reactions to this aggressively male Spaniard.

She had heard once that Spaniards were apt to fall into two distinct types: the tall and the austere who resembled Don Quixote in their looks, and the plump and easily pleased who were more like Don Quixote's servant, Sancho. There was no doubt as to which category Don Joaquin fell into. Judi had a pleasant few moments imagining him tilting at windmills and only stopped when she realised that the windmills had turned into various imaginary women, none of whom had the slightest objection to his attentions.

The episode of the windmills came at the beginning of Cervantes' classic, she remembered. She had given up on the book soon after that, which was probably why it was the only one of Don Quixote's adventures which lingered in her mind. Better not to think of him *or* Don Joaquin. She turned in her seat and smiled at the little girl in the back, solemnly working her way through the box of sweets.

Fabiola, she noticed, had the same high cheekbones as her father, and the same mobile, flyaway eyebrows that were frequently raised in a most effective put-down. She was going to be a beauty one day: she was now, if one didn't think a child's face should be somewhat less well-defined and full of character. Judi's teeth tugged on her lower lip as she compared her own looks with the child's purposeful features. She hadn't much going for her in the beauty stakes, she thought ruefully. A tangle of blond curls topped a wide brow and a face made memorable only by storm-grey eyes and a mouth that curled upwards at the corners, giving her an insouciant, optimistic air that belied what she herself thought of as a singularly prosaic nature. Fabiola had been born to high romance, whereas she and all such flights of fancy would always be strangers. A warm affection for the man she married would be more her style, and that effectively cut out the exotic Don Joaquin.

"Does your grandmother live with you?" she asked the girl.

Fabiola nodded. "Most of the family lives in the castle. We all have separate rooms, you see, though Abuela insists that we all dine with her in the evening. Even Tía Leonor dines with us, though she much prefers not to have to do so. She diets, you know."

Don Joaquin made an impatient sound. "What do you know about Tía Leonor's eating habits?" he demanded of his daughter.

"She's afraid of getting fat. She says Mama let herself go and that one doesn't keep a husband that way. She didn't like Mama."

"Nonsense, child. She's your mother's cousin!"

"She's my cousin, too, and I don't like her much," Fabiola retorted without much interest. "All she can think about is men and what they do. I want to do things myself!"

Don Joaquin quelled his daughter with a frown. "Doña Leonor is a beautiful and cultured woman whom you could well emulate."

"She isn't beautiful," Fabiola said flatly. "She's not beautiful inside."

"That's enough, Fabiola!"

"Sí, Papa."

Judi found her sympathies split both ways. It was plain to see that the unknown Doña Leonor had gone about things in quite the wrong way if she had wanted to make friends with Fabiola, but perhaps it wasn't possible to please both father and daughter at one and the same time.

"Who else lives with you?" Judi asked pacifically.

"Padre Juan de la Cruz. He's Papa's great-uncle. He's a very old man now. He's a priest."

It sounded to Judi like a strange household. She wondered why so many loosely related people should choose to live together. It was a far cry from the small, functional flat she shared with her parents in London. She tried to imagine what it was like to live in a castle and have all one's relations around one all the time.

"Padre Juan takes a deep interest in the new chapel," Don Joaquin warned her. "You'll have to be firm with him if you want to do things your way—as firm as you were with me."

Judi's eyes flew to his face. She couldn't recollect having been particularly firm about anything. If Don Joaquin didn't want her to work for him, he had only to send her home to England. There would be no hard feelings on either side. She was on the point of saying as much when Fabiola spoke from the back. "Padre Juan wants silver nutmegs and golden pears on his vestments. Tía Leonor says he thinks more of the family than he does of the church."

Judi's eyes opened wide with surprised pleasure. "Silver nutmegs and golden pears? Like in the nursery rhyme?"

"What nursery rhyme?" Fabiola demanded, puzzled.

> "*I had a little nut tree.*
> *Nothing would it bear*
> *But a silver nutmeg*
> *And a golden pear;*
> *The King of Spain's daughter*
> *Came to visit me,*
> *And all for the sake*
> *Of my little nut tree.*'"

"What does it mean?" Fabiola asked her, more puzzled still.

"I haven't the faintest idea," Judi confessed. "I always thought it was something to do with a royal marriage. Most nursery rhymes started as political comments on the happenings of the day long ago."

"I think it very silly," said Fabiola.

Judi relapsed into silence. She looked out of the window at the central plain of Spain and wondered at the huge grey boulders that lay scattered across the scrubby land. She knew Don Joaquin was looking at her out of the corner of his eye as he drove the car along the newly resurfaced road and she wished he didn't have the power to make her feel so self-conscious. She had to repress the instinct to put up a hand and straighten her hair, and she found herself hoping that she didn't need to renew her lipstick. She wished that she'd taken time out at the hotel when they had picked up her luggage to make herself more presentable. She felt the colour rise in her cheeks as he went on glancing at her whenever the traffic on the road permitted.

"Is there something wrong?" she asked him.

"No, no. Where did you learn to speak Spanish?"

Had she said something wrong? Had she misinterpreted something?

"At school and at evening classes."

"Ah!" He actually smiled, revealing almost perfect teeth that contrasted with the olive tones of his sunburnt face.

"What does that mean?" she demanded, nettled.

"You have a charming accent. Well done!"

"Haven't all English people?"

He didn't answer her directly. "I like to hear you speak my language. Tell me about yourself."

"There's nothing much to tell."

"Nothing?" His dark eyes mocked her. "There must be something more than that you do embroidery and have come here to dress our family chapel."

"No, really, nothing," she insisted.

"No boyfriend?"

That was a sore point. However, she saw no reason to tell him about her one major romantic adventure to date. David had thought he loved her, but he hadn't. They were both lucky he had found out in time. She had been telling herself that ever since he had asked for his ring back because he had met someone else. That was why it had been such a break for her to come to Spain just now. She could tell herself it was a good thing David was marrying someone else, but she couldn't have borne to have gone to the wedding.

"No, no boyfriend," she said aloud.

Don Joaquin gave her a lazy look. "A cold marriage is worse than none at all. Is that why you came to Spain?"

She held her head up high. "I came because I'm very good at my work and your mother asked me to. I was recommended to her by the School, by the way, so you can see there's nothing personal in it at all."

He smiled for a second time. "We'll have to see what we can do to change that."

"Thank you, but I don't want any changes!" she snapped. "I'm very happy as I am."

"No woman is happy without a man in her life." She saw the flash of amusement in his swiftly veiled eyes and had the uncomfortable feeling he was teasing her.

"Don't flatter yourself, señor. I have other things on my mind right now."

"For now," he repeated, "but how long will that last? Spain will be very good for you, *querida*. It'll teach you much you didn't know about yourself if you think all you want to do all your life is to sew a fine seam."

"*Querida* indeed!" she scoffed. "Keep your endearments for Fabiola! She won't misunderstand them."

"Nor will you," he said softly.

Judi searched her mind for a stinging retort but, before one could occur to her, they turned off the main road as it ran on through the valley ahead of them and began to climb by way of a series of hairpin bends up towards a small town on the brow of the hill.

"That's where we live!" Fabiola told her excitedly. "You see the *alcázar*?"

Judi did indeed. It looked to her like something straight out of Walt Disney, a small pink castle with splendid ramparts and a lot of little pepperpot towers that stood out against the rapidly setting sun. Even as she looked, the security lights came on, making it look more like a figment of her imagination than ever.

"It's beautiful!" she gasped.

"And cold in the winter," her employer warned her. "I hope you have some warm clothes with you."

It seemed no time at all before they drew up beside the ancient drawbridge beside the castle. A woman in black came out to greet them, shivering against the cold breeze of the evening. Belatedly, Judi recognised her as being Don Joaquin's mother.

"What have we here?" the older woman demanded. "It would have been better if you'd arrived tomorrow, señorita, as we arranged. My son has other things to do besides act as chauffeur to a mere employee. Please come inside at once and explain yourself. Fabiola, you may come too. Your father has his own affairs to see to and they don't include you. Follow me."

Fabiola threw Judi a warning glance, but even so Judi couldn't resist looking back towards the car and Don Joaquin. When he raised his hand in salute, she could feel his mother's rigid disapproval coming towards her in waves. What a strange household it was!

Chapter Two

The drawbridge was made of ancient wooden planks, and through the cracks one could see the long drop down to what had once been the moat. Placing her feet with care lest her heels should catch in the spaces, Judi followed Doña Maria into the castle.

"This way," the older woman indicated. She eyed Judi with renewed disapproval. "I can't understand why Fabiola should make so much of your coming to work for us. Have you been bribing the child with sweets?"

Judi merely smiled. "It was the other way round as a matter of fact—"

"It would be! Oh well, you're here now and we must just make the best of it. Once my son gets an idea into his head, there's nothing the rest of us can do about it. I don't suppose he gave a thought as to whether we would be ready to receive you today." She sighed gustily. "No, no, don't apologise, child. I'm sure you had no say in the matter."

Relieved, Judi's smile grew warmer. "Not much," she admitted. "To tell you the truth, I was glad of the lift. I was so surprised to see Fabiola in Avila, and it was nice to be made so welcome."

"She's at a difficult age," her grandmother warned. "She lives with adults far too much, but Don Joaquin won't hear of her being sent away to school as a boarder."

"How old is she?" Judi asked.

"She will soon be twelve. Don't let her run you ragged if you have other things to do. She takes strong likes and dislikes to people and is every bit as stubborn as her father. Let's go into my sitting-room while your rooms are being prepared. Shall I order tea for you?"

Judi thanked her, a little awed by the prospect of actually living in a medieval castle. Yet it didn't look old at all. The rooms they passed through were formally furnished in the Spanish way, but they were warm and the windows were double-glazed against the wintry winds that blew across the central plains of Spain.

Doña Maria's sitting-room was small enough to be cosy. She invited Judi to sit down on one of her English chairs, seating herself opposite her, her back ramrod straight and her hands linked together in her lap.

"I shall be glad when my son marries again," she confided. "Such a responsibility, you know, keeping everything going as he thinks they should be. A younger woman will be able to manage much better. Of course, he's still in mourning for poor Teresa, but as soon as that is over he will have to marry again. He has in mind a very suitable match. You'll probably meet her for yourself while you're here. I can't imagine she'll be interested in the decorations for the chapel, but it would be as well if she were to approve everything before your plans get too far advanced. I know you're to have a free hand, but it would be more tactful, don't you think?"

Judi nodded her head. A *suitable* marriage? She wondered why she should feel hollow inside at the thought. She couldn't imagine that any-one would be able to force Don Joaquin into something he didn't like. With his first wife dead, perhaps he felt that love could never enter his life again. It was a depressing thought. He was so very much alive and his masculinity had been almost tangible to her in the close confines of the car. She caught herself imagining what it would be like to be married to him, and said the first thing that came into her head.

"Does Fabiola like her future stepmother?"

Doña Maria looked decidedly uneasy. "I'm sure she does. A smart young woman is just what she needs to guide her at her age. Of such good family, too. Fabiola doesn't really know her yet. Besides, she'll be growing up and we'll be looking round for a suitable husband for her before we know it!"

"She doesn't like her!" Judi exclaimed.

"I hardly think that is our business—" Doña Maria began.

"No, of course not. I'm sorry," Judi apologised.

"I shouldn't have told you," the older woman

continued, "but it's always better to have these things quite clear from the start. Don Joaquin is a very attractive man, and I shouldn't like you to misunderstand what can only be his friendliness towards all his employees. Spain is not England, my dear."

"No," Judi agreed wryly.

"We don't have your easy approach to marriage and we are far more hot-blooded. The combination isn't always easy to manage, nor for a foreigner to understand."

Judi pulled herself out of her momentary depression. "I didn't come to Spain for romance," she assured Doña Maria.

"Very sensible! Ah, here's tea. Will you have lemon and sugar?"

"Just lemon, thank you." Judi had already given up hope of having milk in her tea until she got back to England. It would be good for her figure, she comforted herself. She tested the tea, found she liked it, and settled herself more comfortably in her chair.

Normally, she would have been amused at being so thoroughly warned off her new employer, but she hardly thought it necessary. True, Don Joaquin was an extremely attractive man, but there was nothing of the siren about her, or so she had always been led to believe.

Once Doña Maria had delivered her warning, however, she disposed herself to be as charming as only a formal Spanish hostess can be, indulging her guest's every whim with a mixture of gentle laughter and undisguised feminine curiosity as to every detail of Judi's family life. Judi was surprised to find how much she had revealed about herself by the time the maid came to escort her to the rooms which had been put aside for her use upstairs.

"Will you forgive me for not coming with you?" Doña Maria asked with a rueful smile. "My arthritis prevents me from moving about as I used to. I find the stairs painful these days."

"Of course," Judi said immediately. "You've been more than kind already."

"If you make our chapel as pretty as Teresa wanted it to be, that'll be enough reward for all of us. Don't hesitate to tell me if you lack anything you need. It might be better not to bother my son with too many of the trivial details, don't you agree?"

Judi didn't think this worthy of an answer. She shook Doña Maria's outstretched hand and thanked her for the tea. She would be glad to get to her room and see where she was to work in the coming weeks. Besides, she was curious to see more of the castle, which she knew dated from the eleventh century. She had never in her wildest dreams imagined herself sleeping in a castle in Spain!

Nor was she disappointed. Her bedroom was situated in one of the towers, looking down on the tops of the trees below, and across the pinkish plain to a typical little group of houses topped with pantiles in which some weeds had taken root, but were dying off now in the cold winds of approaching winter. Further off were some cultivated patches of earth, but she couldn't make out what was growing there. Of the town, of which the castle had once been the main fortress, there was no sign at all. It must lie on the other side of the castle and she was touched that she had been given such a magnificent view for her stay there.

The bedroom had its own bathroom leading off it and, when she tried the second door, she found a workroom had been put at her disposal. She supposed this was normally a bedroom cleared for her use, for the only furniture in it now was a large table and the very latest model of a well-known sewing machine.

The maid had returned to unpack her things when Judi came back to the bedroom. She looked up with a bright smile and hurried across the room to show Judi the concealed wardrobe in the wall, going on to demonstrate the hidden lighting in the glass over the dressing table.

"Doña Maria wishes to know if you'll be eating with the family tonight, or if you'd prefer to have a dish in your room?"

Judi hesitated. Beautiful as her surroundings were, she thought she would have enough of her own company if she were to eat by herself every day.

"What time does the family eat?" she asked.

"Not late," the maid assured her. "Usually at nine o'clock. There is the little one to consider. When there are guests they eat later—at about ten o'clock—but you won't be expected to join them then."

"Could I eat up here tonight? I don't want to make any extra work for you, but it would be nice just this once."

"It'll be a pleasure, señorita. You must be tired from travelling and you'll want an early night. I'll bring your food at seven and then, if you wish an early night, there will be nothing to disturb you."

It struck Judi as strange that a meal timed for nine could be brought to her at seven. She had not yet experienced the tepid food that is tolerated as a feature of Spanish cuisine, served on cold plates, carried long distances from far-off kitchens as a matter of course and frequently prepared in the dining room hours before it would be needed, or whenever the cook had a moment to spare from her other engrossing activities.

As soon as the maid had gone, there was another knock at the door. Judi paused in the removal of her jacket and went to answer it. Outside stood a rotund little priest with a bald head and a sweet smile.

"Señorita Hudi? I am Padre Juan de la Cruz, the uncle of Doña Maria. I'm retired from active parish work nowadays and my nephew allows me to live here as chaplain to the family. I came to show you the chapel." His enthusiasm shone out of his eyes. "I thought you'd want to see it immediately," he almost pleaded with her.

"Yes, of course," Judi responded at once, putting aside her weariness. The priest would be a useful ally, she thought, and besides, she liked him enough to think she might be able to try out her own ideas on him before submitting them to Don Joaquin.

The priest rubbed his hands together in glee. "My hobby is heraldry, señorita. This family has many emblems which you'd find useful as motifs, no?"

Judi had thought to decorate the vestments with the various symbols of suitable saints and she told him so. "Your niece told me she wanted them simple and modern."

"Yes, yes, indeed! But what is more simple than a few silver nutmegs and some golden pears? You'll find them on all the family's heraldic devices. Perhaps on the altar linen?"

Judi was amused. "Perhaps," she admitted.

Padre Juan was quick to press home his advantage. "You have a free hand, I know. You must do what you think best. Have you a device of your own you'd like included?"

Judi shook her head. "I don't come from that sort of family, Padre."

He looked surprised. "I've heard you are all very modern in England," he comforted her.

"You don't understand," she insisted gently. "My family has *never* had any noble blood in it."

Padre Juan looked amazed. "In Spain, every man is a king!" he claimed.

Judi didn't doubt that was so. She had already discovered the impossibility of offering advice to any Spanish male. She remembered a diminutive waiter who had barely started school and had wanted to pour her out a measure of brandy in a glass designed for a litre of beer. She had pointed out that his family wouldn't make much profit out of his largesse, only to be told that his family was not as mean as she supposed. They could well afford to show their approval of a pretty woman!

The chapel was a large, oblong room. At one end, approached by two steps, was the core of the altar which, one day, like the floor and steps, would be covered by marble, but which was now bare, dusty concrete. Only the windows were finished, coloured in dazzling blues and reds, and a small tomb, covered in white marble and bearing the legend in gold: M. TERESA ZAM- ARRALA.

"You see how much there is to be done!" the priest exclaimed.

But Judi was scarcely listening to him. Her mind was busily considering colours and de- signs for the vestments and altar linen that she would be responsible for designing and execut- ing.

"What colours will the marble be?" she asked.

"White. All white, edged with green marble from Italy. All the seats will need to be covered when they arrive. It's a great work you've under- taken!"

"Don't frighten the poor girl before she's even got started, Padre," Don Joaquin drawled from the doorway.

Judi turned to face him, the blood draining from her face. The sight of him made her heart beat faster and her mouth was suddenly dry. Her tongue felt like a lump of wood, making it impos- sible for her to swallow.

"I'm looking forward to having Padre Juan's advice," she said stiffly.

Don Joaquin's gaze was amused. His eyes rested for a long moment on her lips, falling to the curve of her breasts which betrayed her quickened breathing. "Does the prospect of de- signing the accoutrements of a chapel excite you, señorita?" he asked.

"I enjoy my work, yes," she answered cau- tiously.

He came and stood beside her, putting a hand on her shoulder and forcing her to take a step towards the white marble tomb.

"*She* is the one you have to please. Remember that."

"Your wife?" she whispered.

"The little one's mother," Padre Juan interposed.

Judi stared down at the simple grave. "You haven't given her her married name," she observed at last.

The priest shook his head at her. "She had her own name. Sometimes, for social convenience, a woman will be called by her husband's name, but legally she retains her own." He sighed. "These old ways are going now. I find it a pity."

Don Joaquin's hand tightened its hold on her shoulder. "Don't you want to keep your own name when you marry?" he mocked her.

"I've never thought about it." Her flesh burned beneath his touch and she was very aware of the strength of his body beside hers. She tried to move away from him, pulling at his hand with hers.

"No boyfriend and no thoughts of marriage?" Don Joaquin murmured, his face close to hers. He took her hand in his and examined it carefully. "No rings either?"

She twisted her hand in his. "Please let me go!"

"Don't you like to have your hand kissed?"

"We don't go in for it much in England!" she rounded on him.

A smile played on his lips. "In Spain we do. Haven't you noticed that our women wear their

33

wedding rings on their right hand? We kiss it to show we respect their married state. Now what is there to disapprove of in that?"

"Nothing," Judi was forced to agree. "Except I'm not a married lady!"

"So I shall have to think of some other excuse to kiss your hand. What would you suggest?"

Judi looked round to gain Padre Juan's support, but the priest had slipped out from the chapel and she was quite alone with Don Joaquin. She didn't know if she was glad or sorry, but she was sure it would be dangerous to linger too long in his company.

"I suggest you let me go!" she said firmly.

His eyes looked deep into hers. "Why aren't you eating with us this evening?"

"I'm tired. I wanted an early night."

"Then I'll escort you back to your room. It's easy to get lost—until you're used to the castle." He bent his head, brushing his lips against hers. "How come you have no boyfriend back in England?"

Judi trembled inwardly. She was shocked by how much she wanted him to kiss her properly, though she hardly thought a chapel a proper place for it. Then she laughed at herself for having such an English reaction, seizing on the notion to divert her mind away from the effect Don Joaquin was having on her.

"Are your English men blind to the charms of a pretty girl?" Don Joaquin went on, wondering at the smile that trembled on her lips.

"Do Spaniards always flirt with people they've only just met?" she retorted.

"I want you to feel at home here," he explained, patting her cheek.

Feel at home! What kind of a life did he think she had led in England that she should be so in need of masculine attention? Didn't he realise she was a staid creature at heart? David had frequently complained that she never lost her head or got excited about anything—

She felt a blush begin to rise into her cheeks. If the pounding of her heart was anything to go by, she was right now a long way from being the calm, cool girl of yesterday.

"I'd feel more at home if you kept your distance," she said more sharply than she had intended.

He stood back from her, surveying her from head to foot, his eyes enigmatic. "Very well," he said at last. "I'll take you to your room."

Judi was unprepared for the wave of disappointment that washed over her. She had been enjoying the exchange, she realised with a small gasp at the back of her throat. She felt more fully alive than she had since David had told her he was in love with someone else. Convinced that she wouldn't care, he had told her in an off-hand manner, she remembered. Perhaps she *hadn't* cared enough, she thought now. She had never been as aware of him—or of any man—as she was of this comparative stranger who walked silently beside her through the castle to her room.

"Good night, señor," she said at her door.

"Good night, *pequeña*. Sweet dreams."

She hesitated in the doorway, unwilling to spend the evening by herself after all. "Will you want to see my designs yourself?" she asked him, trying to keep him a little longer.

His sardonic smile told her he had read her

mind. *"Buenas noches,* señorita. We can talk about work in the morning, or have you forgotten you're tired and longing for your bed?"

"Good night," she said again.

Inside her room, with the door shut, she took herself to task for dallying with him. He would think she wanted him to flirt with her! She had come to Spain to work and to give her bruised heart space to recover from David's defection, not to feel fully female for the first time in her life, nor to have her blood dance through her veins for a man who had made one suitable marriage and was about to make another! She had other, better things to think about. Only, it was a pity how dull they suddenly seemed and not worth thinking about at all.

All in all, it was a relief when the maid came with her food and turned down her bed, ready for her to get into. Judi was glad to discover that all that was the matter with her was that she was hungry. She didn't care if the food was stone cold and she was unaccustomed to taking wine with her meals. Nevertheless, she ate and drank with a healthy gusto, putting the empty tray outside her door for the maid to collect later.

Don Joaquin seemed much less dangerous to her peace of mind by the time she was ready to go to sleep. What was he, after all? Only a man. Only one more man to be taken or left alone in her usual calm manner. And on that thought she slept.

The sun was shining. Judi leapt out of bed and went to stand by the window, a breath of excitement passing through her as she remembered that she was in a castle in Spain and that she was here to work. She wasn't just visiting the castle, she had a right to be here. For the next few weeks it was going to be home to her, with its turret rooms and twisty staircases and the large, formal rooms down below looking like something out of a medieval film.

She glanced at her watch without really looking at it. Surely she had time to explore the immediate vicinity if she hurried. She was almost sure there would be nobody about, not even the maids. If the last meal had been at nine o'clock, nobody would want breakfast before eight. She glanced at her watch again and saw it was nearly that now. It was hard to remember that Spain, although as far west as Great Britain, ran on mid-European time in the winter. If it had been as early as she had first thought, the sun wouldn't have risen yet. With such dark mornings it was no wonder that everyone slept on.

Once dressed, she let herself out of her bedroom and took the first staircase downstairs, descending into a room of enormous proportions which she took to be a ballroom of some sort, though it was difficult to see, for such furniture as there was, lined up round the mirrored walls, was covered by a variety of dust-sheets. Out of this room was a smaller withdrawing room, furnished by a single French gilt table, the surface of which was taken up by a trio of dancing cherubs. It was decorative but hardly practical, and Judi disliked it on sight. Hurrying away from it, she found herself in yet another room, this time a hallway that led out through some French doors to a closed-in verandah.

She tried the handle, half expecting to find the

doors locked, but they opened to her touch and she stepped out onto the verandah, walking across to the ancient wall, now topped by double-glazing, from where she could see right across the valley below.

"*Buenos días,* señorita!"

Judi gasped, turned to look towards where the voice had come from and prepared to run back the same way she had come. She wasn't ready to meet Don Joaquin so early in the morning. She had planned to do a great deal of work on her designs before seeing him again. When they were discussing her work they met on equal terms and she needed the security her work gave her. It was ridiculous to be rendered immobile by the mere sight of him, but she couldn't bring herself to move in any direction as Don Joaquin rose slowly to his feet, gesturing towards the table set for breakfast before him.

"Come and join me," he invited her. "Will you have coffee? Or do you prefer to begin your day with hot chocolate?"

Judi knew she was going to stammer as she answered him and took an indignant breath, cross with herself for her lack of control.

"N-neither. Please go on with your breakfast, señor. I didn't mean to disturb you. I didn't think anyone else was up yet."

He drew out a chair for her, ignoring her protests. "Fabiola sometimes joins me for breakfast. The rest of the family prefer to get up after they've eaten. Sit down, Hudi, and don't be silly. I won't eat you!"

But he did bother her. She could feel his breath against her cheek as he put her chair into the table before sitting down again himself. His

movements were lithe and agile and she could
see his muscles ripple under the close-fit of his
shirt. She looked away hastily lest he should
notice her interest and draw his own, disastrous,
conclusions.

"I think your mother would prefer that I didn't
breakfast with you," she said aloud.

"Fortunately my mother no longer governs my
actions," he returned lazily. His eyes rested
lightly on her face. "You are *my* employee, señorita, not my mother's, just as the whole castle
belongs to me and everything that goes on inside
it is my responsibility. Remember that."

She stirred in her seat, not knowing quite how
to answer him. "Your mother—" she began.

"—will quite understand," he finished for her.
A mocking smile touched the corners of his lips.
"*Sí*, señor," he prompted her.

"*Sí*, señor," she repeated rebelliously. Now,
she thought, was not the moment to fight with
him. It was not even the moment to point out
that she had no intention of being pushed into a
corner by either him or his mother. That would
come in time when they had had a chance to
realise the value of her work and that she was
something more than a young girl who could be
used as a pawn in anyone's game.

Chapter Three

Don Joaquin spoke rapidly to the maid now standing by the French doors. She disappeared into the house and came back almost immediately with some sweet orange jam in her hand.

"We want you to feel at home here," her employer told her. "I had my mother get in some marmalade especially for you. All English people eat marmalade for breakfast."

This was marmalade? Judi hid a smile. Here she was, in the home of the Seville orange, and the only use they had for its bitter taste was to plant them in public places to ensure that nobody picked the fruit.

"How kind," she said aloud, spreading her freshly baked bread with a scraping of the jam.

Don Joaquin smiled with satisfaction. "I'm glad you're pleased." He leaned back in his chair, studying her through half-closed eyes. "Are your rooms comfortable?"

Judi nodded. "There's a splendid view from the windows!" she exclaimed. "I'm afraid it'll prove to be quite a distraction when I start work."

"You take your work very seriously, don't you?"

"Is there any reason why I shouldn't?" she countered.

"No, no, it's fitting work for a woman," he returned dismissively. "Why did you choose it? Don't most girls want to become a secretary, or a nurse, or something like that?"

"Would you believe I chose it because I'm good at it?"

He was amused. "That good?"

"That good," she assured him solemnly.

"You should learn to play a little, Hudi. You think too much of your needle and thread."

She opened her eyes very wide, mocking him as he had her. "I came to Spain to work," she told him. "As my employer you should be glad of that."

"As a man I could wish it were otherwise."

She glanced at him sharply, but he was no longer looking at her. His face was innocent of all expression and, for a brief instant, she thought she had imagined the remark. Her knife slipped on her plate, falling to the floor, and she bent to pick it up, glad of the excuse to conceal her heightened colour.

His hand met hers under the table and his fingers grasped hers for an instant, giving them a quick squeeze before she surfaced again. He returned her knife to her with a courteous, very continental bow.

"Thank you," she murmured, distracted by the tingling sensation in her fingers where he had held them.

"*De nada*. Tell me about this man you are running away from. Is he the fool I think he is to allow you to get away so easily?"

She wasn't going to answer. He had no business to be asking such questions and she meant to tell him so. Apparently he had the idea that no woman could function adequately without the proper guidance of some male.

"He married someone else," she said abruptly. "Satisfied?"

Don Joaquin frowned. "Didn't your father find out if he were serious before you got involved with him?"

"My father," Judi said in withering tones, "wasn't thinking of marrying him."

Don Joaquin shrugged. "At least we've established the man to be a fool. You are better off without him. One can only be glad he had enough sense to marry someone else."

"That's what I keep telling myself," Judi confessed dryly.

His expression softened. "Doesn't it work?"

"In patches. A change of scene makes it easier."

"Another man in your life would make it easier still, don't you think?"

"No, I don't," Judi said coldly. "All I want is to be left alone to get on with my work. Shall we change the subject?"

"If you insist." He smiled slowly. "Your work

won't be enough for you for long, *hermosa mía.*
Any man who's kissed you could tell you that."

Judi sucked in her breath, wishing her heart
would keep still. How dare he call her beautiful?
And he with one wife dead and shortly to be
engaged to another! Did he think himself irre-
sistible? Well, perhaps he had cause for that.
She couldn't imagine many women turning him
down, which was all the more reason for her to
make it clear that she wasn't about to become
one of his victims. She could refuse his advanc-
es only too easily. After all, he was still a complete stranger to her.

"They won't get the chance!" she said grimly.

"No? Are your defences so impregnable?"

"Yes they are!" she snapped.

"I wonder," he mused. "I wonder that very
much." He leaned forward suddenly, catching
her off-balance. "I could kiss you if I chose—as I
did last night. It would be the quickest way for
you to forget your errant lover!"

She bit her lip. "You have your own affairs to
worry about, señor. I'm sure mine aren't really
of any interest to you. I believe I have to congratulate you on your forthcoming marriage.
Wouldn't it be better if you kept your romantic
offers for her?"

The laughter drained from his face. "My
mother has been talking to you? It's true she
wishes me to marry again but she shouldn't take
too much for granted. I made one marriage to
please my family; my next, if there is one, will
be to please myself."

"What about Fabiola?" Judi dared to ask.

Don Joaquin's face was a mask. He nodded

slowly. "Fabiola needs a younger woman to help her grow up," he acknowledged. "My mother is too old to cope with her every day. She gets tired these days." He cast Judi a swift, sideways glance that was full of charm, a charm she was aware of in every inch of her body. "If I were to ask a favour of you, little Hudi, would you claim you had more than enough to do with this work of yours?"

Judi wanted to do just that, but she could feel herself weakening despite herself. When he looked at her like that, her insides turned to warm treacle. Blast him! She didn't want to get involved with him, not through Fabiola, and not in any other way!

"Isn't Fabiola a good reason for you to marry again?" she found herself suggesting.

"Fabiola doesn't much care for my mother's choice of bride," he answered dryly. "She's had my attention all to herself since her mother died and she resents the thought of another woman in her mother's place, yet she needs to learn from someone how to be a woman herself. She can't command armies all her life. While you are here, will you try to show her the attractions of some gentler pursuits? It's too much to hope that she will willingly sit and embroider or sew a fine seam, but she could learn to choose her own clothes and that to be a girl is not something to be despised. Her grandmother has very old-fashioned ideas and it's not surprising the child should rebel against them. Would you mind doing that for me, Hudi?"

"She wants to be like you," Judi murmured. "What was her mother like?" As soon as the words were out, she wished them unsaid. She had no right to ask him such a personal question. Though when she thought of how he had asked her about David, she couldn't help thinking that perhaps he had given her that right.

"She was beautiful in a gentle, ineffective way that hid a will of steel. She had a vocation to the religious life, but her family would have none of it. She married me out of obedience to their wishes and we both regretted it from then on. Many young girls pass through a phase when they think they want to be nuns, and then, when they marry, they transfer all that feeling to their husbands and families. Teresa was the exception. Her marriage interfered with her prayers and, after Fabiola's birth, she withdrew from life more and more until she finally died. It was what she wanted. She made me promise to marry again for Fabiola's sake, to be the mother to her that she never was, but—"

"Didn't you love her at all?" Judi asked, appalled by the picture he had drawn.

"Not as most men love their wives. I was fond of her and I thought I would grow to love her in marriage. I loved her as one loves a saint, as did everyone else around her. She had no enemies and few friends. She was totally absorbed in God."

Judi didn't know what to say to that. It was hard to imagine that any woman married to Don Joaquin could have been as indifferent as he had made his dead wife out to be. She tried not to think how she would have reacted under the same circumstances. Would she have preferred him not to make love to her? The fluttering of her heart denied it for her. She could imagine herself hating Don Joaquin—or loving him—but never turning her back on him for her prayers.

"Poor Fabiola," she said at last. "I see why your mother wants you to marry again."

Don Joaquin lifted an eyebrow. "Can you? Well, I might come to it yet, but this time it'll be to a woman who'll meet me halfway, a woman who likes to make love and isn't ashamed to show it."

"A hot-blooded, Spanish woman," Judi put in, wondering why the idea should be an affront to her.

"Leonor is hot-blooded enough," he agreed slowly. "Perhaps I'm asking too much to seek for other qualities as well."

"Why don't you settle for love?" Judi demanded. "Or is that too simple a need for you?"

"Will you marry for love?" he questioned her, his eyes alight with a curiosity about her which she couldn't understand.

"Or not at all," she nodded.

"Ah, but how to find love? You won't find it hiding yourself away in Spain. To find love you have to take a chance. I think you're too much of a coward to win in the love stakes, *pequeña,* if you won't allow a man to kiss you, or come near you."

"I won't allow *you*—"

"Nor any other man under my roof!"

She didn't care for the proprietorial note in his voice. She lifted her chin and returned his fierce look with interest. "Isn't that for me to say?" she said gently.

He frowned at her. "You have no more idea of what goes on in a man's mind than Fabiola has."

"I was engaged to be married!"

"But you've never known love, as anyone can see by looking at you. You're untried and untouched by your ex-fiancé or any other man. Love can hurt as much as it heals. It can be a violent storm or a gentle breeze. You have never experienced either." He spread his hands in a very Spanish gesture. "Didn't I tell you the man's a fool?"

Judi gave him a bitter look. "I'm surprised you want me to take an interest in Fabiola if you think I've no more sense than she has," she observed painfully.

He smiled slowly. "I've offended you? You should be glad you escaped so lightly from such a dull affair of the heart. You owe him neither love nor loyalty, and that's a good thing, isn't it?"

"I thought I loved him. I *did* love him!" Judi claimed.

"And I say you did not. Shall I prove it to you?"

Judi tried to speak, but the words stuck in the back of her throat. She thought it very likely that he was teasing her in a strange way that she couldn't understand. How could anyone prove such a thing to her? Only she knew how she had felt about David—how she felt about him still.

Don Joaquin took her hand in his, drawing her to her feet and guiding her into the circle of his arms. She had only to step away from him and she would break the spell, she told herself, but she knew she had no intention of doing anything of the sort. There was a light in his eyes that destroyed her willpower and turned her knees to water. She had said she didn't want to be kissed by him, and she had very nearly persuaded herself that she had been speaking the truth, but now she knew she had lied. She wanted him to kiss her more than she had ever wanted anything from a man before. Her whole body ached with her need to feel his lips against hers.

Even so, nothing had prepared her for his kiss when it came. He was very gentle, putting his lips to hers and holding her with no more pressure than it took to keep her close up against him. For an instant she was disappointed and she swallowed convulsively at the lump in her throat, betraying her uncertainty and her guilty thought that she ought to walk away from him while she still could.

Then her whole world spun about her and she was as much a prisoner to herself as she was to him. Her mouth opened beneath his and her arms crept up round the back of his head to feel the hard muscles of his neck, shoulders and down his back to his hips. His own hold tightened on her, his kiss deepening and becoming more demanding of a corresponding response from her. She could deny him nothing. She was aware of the tang of his after-shave, and then she could think of nothing except that she had never been kissed like this before. His hands found her breasts and undid the buttons of her shirt to make the contact closer still.

It was he who broke the kiss, soothing her with a gentle, stroking motion before he rebuttoned her shirt and put her away from him.

"You're too beautiful for me not to want more than a few kisses from you," he sighed, "and you're not ready for anything else, are you?"

Her head drooped against his shoulder. "I

don't know," she said, bewildered by the strength of her own emotions.

"That's for a husband and marriage. At least now you'll be able to forget your heartbreak over your ex-fiancé, no?"

David? Her cheeks burned with a sudden embarrassment. How could she have thought that she loved him? But worse, far worse, how could she have allowed Don Joaquin to expose her feelings to her own eyes and to his in this wanton manner. A burning anger replaced her previous emotions, an anger with herself but even more with him. He had known what he was doing; she had not.

"If you've finished your fun and games, I have work to do!" she informed him with a toss of her head. "And in future, keep your hands to yourself!"

His look was quizzical. "Do you want me to apologise?"

"*No!*" The question stung as she suspected it was meant to do. She already knew that she had kissed him every bit as much as he had kissed her. The only difference was that her regret was genuine, whereas his— He didn't look as though he regretted the incident at all! On the contrary, he looked remarkably pleased with himself. *Smug!*

"That's just as well. I'd find it hard to apologise for anything so delightful."

"Delightful to whom?"

"To both of us, *pequeña*, as you very well know!"

"Not to me! I feel cheap and—and—"

He shook his head, his eyes laughing at her,

though not unkindly. "You are quite safe with me. I won't hurt you, little Hudi. I thought it time for you to know that this other man meant nothing to you—"

"What business is it of yours?" Judi stormed, her humiliation complete. He hadn't even *wanted* to kiss her! He was being kind. And it wasn't his *kindness* that she wanted. She had forgotten all about his plans for remarriage. She had forgotten everything while in his arms, except that it had felt right to be there and she had wanted him to go on kissing her forever.

He stroked her cheek with his forefinger, smiling when she slapped his hand away from her face.

"An attractive girl is of interest to every man. Make friends with Fabiola and be happy while you're amongst us in Spain. You're too young to run away from life—and too much alive to succeed!"

So that was what he thought of her. A child like Fabiola! She didn't know why the knowledge should hurt her, but she felt rubbed raw and of no significance to anyone.

"You should have left well enough alone," she told him flatly. "If you're expecting my thanks, I'm not in the least bit grateful. I dislike you more than I can say!"

His eyes narrowed. "Don't tempt me, Hudi, or I may do something yet that we'll both regret."

"And don't call me Hudi! My name is Judi, not that I've asked you to call me by it. Miss Duggan is what I'd prefer."

He considered the matter, laughing at her. "Too formal," he decided. "Hudi is more friendly. Or *palomita,* or *bombón—*"

Outraged, she turned on him. "If those mean what I think they mean, you'd better not let anyone else hear you call me such silly names!"

"They suit you," he assured her. "I suppose the equivalent in English is dove, or sweetie. Haven't you ever been called by a pet name before?"

"Certainly not!"

"Then it's time you were. You may even grow to like it if you give yourself a chance." He sketched a salute, smiling broadly. "I could waste a great deal more time with you, but I must get to work, *preciosa*. Shall I see you at breakfast tomorrow?"

It was the last straw as far as Judi was concerned. He hadn't even allowed her to be the one to bring the interview to an end. She hadn't even had that satisfaction. If he had work to do, so had she. She should have walked away from him much earlier, she realised belatedly. She should never have even risked joining him for breakfast.

"Don't let me keep you!" she shot back at him.

"There'll be other days when I won't have to leave you," he comforted her.

"Then I'll leave you!"

"I wonder," he drawled. *"Hasta luego!"*

"Adiós," she responded formally.

The sun went in as soon as he had gone. Judi reflected bleakly that he probably had control over the elements too, knowing that she would wish the sun back again. She would *not* wish him back though, never, never, *never!* But it was dull without him and she didn't feel in the least like going upstairs and starting work.

She went anyway. The maid had been in and

had made her bed, and she told herself that another time she would have to remember to make it before she left her bedroom. The girl had enough to do without waiting on her hand and foot.

The workroom felt empty. Judi spread her papers around on the top of the working table and sighed over the quantities of vestments that would be needed, one set in each of the liturgical colours, perhaps more if other priests were to celebrate Mass in the family chapel. Oh well, she would begin with Padre Juan. She had to start somewhere.

Her first drawings were as bad as she had feared they would be. She looked at them with distaste, despising herself for allowing Don Joaquin to unsettle her so thoroughly. With him, it would be out of sight, out of mind; why couldn't it be like that with her? She looked down at the sheet of paper she was working on and was horrified to see Don Joaquin's masculine features looking back at her. She tore the paper in two, screwed it up into a little ball and cast it into the wastepaper basket, where it ricocheted round the top and fell out again. She stood up to put it where it belonged just as there was a sharp knock on the door.

"*Adelante,*" she called out.

The door was flung open to reveal a perfectly posed, strange young woman, her head thrown back and one hand on hip.

"Hullo there," the young woman said in husky tones.

Judi straightened her back slowly, fascinated by this vision. Her visitor's hair had been dyed a bright orange and she was wearing a dress to match. Her brows were black, and her eyes so pale they were scarcely visible at all. By contrast, Judi felt plain and ordinary in her workmanlike grey pantsuit edged in scarlet, with a white blouse which Don Joaquin had lent, crumpled and with the buttons at odds with their corresponding holes.

"Hullo," said Judi.

"I thought I'd come and see how you're getting on. Doña Maria told me you were here. She thought I ought to introduce myself."

Judi removed some drawing paper from the one and only chair. "Won't you sit down?" she invited.

"I'm Teresa's cousin Leonor." She drifted across the room and sat down, crossing her legs in front of her in a studied movement which enabled her to admire her ankles, which she did for a long moment, while Judi stood and waited. "You may call me Leonor," the woman continued finally. "What do I call you?"

"I'm Judi Duggan."

Leonor's tongue tripped over the unaccustomed syllables and she trilled a little laugh. "I shall call you Hudi as Fabiola does. Surely no one can pronounce such a name?"

Judi wrote it down for her, saying it again more slowly, but Leonor had already lost interest. It seemed she was to be Hudi to all and sundry.

"You've met Don Joaquin?" the other woman asked her.

"He drove me here from Avila yesterday."

"Ah yes, with Fabiola. A tiresome little girl, don't you think? So unlike her dear mama. She has far too much energy for any one person. It's no wonder she's too much for her grandmother to cope with. That's what I'm doing here. I felt obliged to come and lend a hand when Doña Maria asked me to. I am a close relation, after all. The family is still in mourning for poor Teresa—Don Joaquin insists on observing all the niceties for a full year, which is a bit excessive for these days, but with these old families they always worry what other people will think. There was enough gossip when Teresa was alive. We all felt so sorry for Joaquin."

Judi smiled determinedly. "Teresa sounds like a lovely person," she said.

"Oh, she was. But she was no wife for a man as virile as Joaquin! He won't make that mistake a second time."

It was no more than Don Joaquin had told her himself, but Judi resented hearing it again from the full-blown lips of Leonor.

"Actually," Leonor went on, apparently not noticing Judi's silence, "we're in much the same line of business. I'm a fashion model. Doña Maria thought I might be able to help you with your designs. What are you working on?"

"I haven't begun yet."

Leonor peered into the wastepaper basket. "What are these? Come on, show me. They'll give me some idea of what you have in mind."

"No, they won't. They're just used up bits of paper. I was thinking some gothic-style vestments might be nice, worked with silver and gold embroidery—"

"Nutmegs and pears?" Leonor interrupted her with a wry smile. "I can see Padre Juan has been talking to you. You know, some priests aren't wearing the full bit these days. They have much wider, ornate stoles instead—so much more sensible in the heat of summer."

"I could do some designs for both," Judi said doubtfully.

"Do that! As soon as you have some ideas on paper, bring them to me and I'll vet them for you before anyone else in the family sees them."

Judi was even more doubtful about that. "Padre Juan—"

"Won't be here much longer, though I'm telling you that in strict confidence. Doña Maria and I have great ideas about the changes we'll make when Joaquin finally comes out of mourning. He's bound to marry to please his family. His mother is very persuasive. Teresa was her choice, you know. Our families have always been closely connected and, naturally, we want that connection to continue. Padre Juan is old and depressing. His sermons are a dead bore. I couldn't stand them week after week for what may be years, so he'll have to go and bore someone else. Then there's Fabiola—" She picked up one of Judi's crayons and tapped her teeth thoughtfully. "I think a boarding school would suit Fabiola's temperament better, don't you? I'm sure I can persuade Doña Maria that Joaquin will be much happier with her out of the way."

"Will Doña Maria go on living here?" Judi couldn't resist asking, a dry note entering her voice which she hoped Leonor wouldn't notice, though there was little danger of that.

"Oh, she's getting to be an old lady. She won't live forever. I daresay she'll do the decent thing and die before long. She's had the best part of her life and can't have much to look forward to."

She shrugged elegant shoulders. "My life is just beginning. With my flair and Joaquin's money, I plan to be one of the best-known people in Europe!"

Poor Fabiola! Judi thought. She preferred not to think about Don Joaquin at all. Then, as if conjured up by the force of Judi's sympathy for her, Fabiola herself came running into the room, her velvet dress askew and her hair a mass of tangles on her shoulders.

"Hudi, Hudi, you're to leave what you're doing at once! Papa says that if you can make me look respectable—" The child's eyes fell on Leonor and the joy left her face. "What is *she* doing here?" she demanded.

"She?" Judi rebuked her mildly. "Tía Leonor kindly came to give me the benefit of her advice."

Fabiola's eyes sparkled with laughter and, for an instant, Judi was afraid she would reveal the cutting underside of her remark to the blithely unaware Leonor. She had underrated Fabiola, however. She turned to her cousin with a grave face.

"I expect Abuela sent you?" she remarked politely. She turned back to Judi. "Papa says he'll take us to Segovia with him if you'll do something about my appearance. He says I look as though I've slept in this dress. Will you, Hudi? Please say yes. He hardly ever takes me anywhere, and we can only go today if you'll come too."

"I could go with you," Leonor suggested tautly.

Fabiola shook her head. "It has to be Hudi

because she won't leave me on my own. *Please,* Hudi, will you?"

Judi ignored the delighted leap of her heart, and smiled. "I'd love to go with you, but only if you'll help me when we get home."

"*Me?*" said Fabiola, astonished. "I don't know anything about sewing."

"You can tell me what your mother would have liked to see in the chapel. Your father—"

"Oh yes, I can tell you that," Fabiola agreed amiably. "Papa and I both know exactly what she would have liked, better than anyone else." She ignored Leonor's furious face with a slight shrug of her shoulders. "Will you please hurry up, Hudi? Papa won't wait for us forever!"

"I'm coming," said Judi, and allowed herself to be dragged along at a run to Fabiola's bedroom at the other end of the castle.

Chapter Four

Judi was dismayed to see the full extent of Fabiola's wardrobe. Everything she had would have been more suitable for a female version of Little Lord Fauntleroy, with velvet, lace collars and bows of hideous colours to be fastened at the neck by means of a safety pin.

"They're awful, aren't they?" Fabiola condemned them, wrinkling up her nose. "I'm not allowed to choose my own clothes. Abuela says I'm too young to know what's suitable."

And Doña Maria was too old, Judi groaned inwardly. Not too old in years, perhaps, but in her ideas.

"Find me a needle and thread and I'll make this fit you better," she commanded.

"We haven't time, Hudi. Papa—"

"Your father will just have to wait."

Recognising that Judi was determined, Fab-

iola rushed away and came back with her grandmother's needlework basket. Judi ruthlessly
slashed away at the dress, bidding Fabiola to
take off the one she was wearing. In a matter of
minutes she had removed most of the bows and
furbelows, revealing the simple basic lines of
the dress.

"Try that," she said.

Fabiola pulled it over her head with impatient hands. "It doesn't matter, Hudi. All my
frocks—" She caught sight of herself in the
glass and broke off, her mouth still open. "It
looks *lovely!*" she approved. "How clever you
are!"

"It'll look better when your hair's done," Judi
said critically.

"It's fantastic!"

"More you?" Judi teased her.

Fabiola grinned happily. "I'd prefer something
like what you're wearing. You look much nicer
than Tía Leonor. She always looks like a stage
prop with that horrid hair."

"That's part of her job," Judi defended her.

"She hasn't got a job. She used to do a photo-
graphic session sometimes when Mama was
alive. Now she lives here free and doesn't have
to work. She wants to live here forever and
ever!"

"It was kind of her to help out your
grandmother—"

"She's bird-witted!"

"She's kinder than you are," Judi retorted
firmly, wishing it were true. "My mother used to
say that if you can't say something kind about a
person, don't say anything at all. It's very good
advice."

"But she is bird-witted. She never thinks of anything except how she looks and whether men think she's beautiful. Haven't you noticed?"

"Your grandmother likes her."

"She wouldn't if she knew that the only thing she likes about Papa is his money!"

"Fabiola!"

"It's true! I always speak the truth."

Judi was afraid that was only too true. She looked helplessly down at the top of Fabiola's head, set at an arrogant angle on her shoulders.

"Silence can be better than the truth, *chica*. Didn't your mother teach you that?"

Fabiola grimaced at herself in the glass. "She tried. She hardly ever spoke at all. It didn't make me feel uncomfortable when she didn't talk though; I knew she liked my being there. Some people you have to talk to all the time in case they think you haven't noticed they're there. Mama wouldn't have minded if you hadn't noticed. She didn't like a lot of attention. Papa wishes I were more like her."

Judi finished brushing the child's hair. "You're too much your father's daughter ever to be ignored!"

Fabiola was pleased with that. "Nobody ever ignores Papa," she agreed complacently. *"Es todo hombre!"*

Judi opened her eyes wide. "What do you know about it?" she teased.

"I am Spanish, like him," Fabiola answered simply. "But you think so too, don't you?"

Judi refused to commit herself either way. "I think you're ready at last," she said instead. "Shall we go?"

Don Joaquin had driven the car up to the front

of the castle and was seated in the driver's seat, waiting for them. He got out when he saw them coming and opened the two doors for them on the right-hand side.

"I told you a quarter-of-an-hour," he began to chide his daughter before he had really seen her. Then he noticed her altered dress and smooth, shiny hair and handed her into the back seat with the same formality he would have extended to his mother. "It was worth waiting to see you looking so pretty," he congratulated her. "Is this Hudi's work?"

Fabiola nodded happily. "She looks pretty, too, doesn't she?"

Judi blushed under his narrowed gaze, pulling the edges of her jacket together in front of her in a defensive gesture. She had been dreading this moment all the time she had been helping Fabiola to dress, but she had not expected to feel this dry-mouthed shyness, nor that she would be so aware of him physically. Even though he didn't touch her, she could still feel the imprint of his fingers against her flesh.

She hurried into the front passenger seat, pulling the door shut behind her with a bang. He opened it again and shut it more gently, pushing the corner of her jacket inside against her thigh.

"More haste, less speed," he mocked her.

Judi searched in her handbag for her lipstick to give herself something to do while he got in beside her. She looked away from him, her fingers trembling as she applied the lipstick with a generous hand. She should never have agreed to come!

He put a hand on her elbow and she winced away from him. "Thank you, Hudi."

Judi huddled against the door. "You're going to have a beauty on your hands when she's older," she forced herself to say. Her voice sounded rusty and out of gear.

"Two beauties won't be too many for me to handle," he murmured with a slanting smile.

Did he see Leonor as beautiful? Judi couldn't agree with him. She shared Fabiola's reservations where that young woman was concerned. She remembered Fabiola saying that she wasn't beautiful inside, but perhaps a man didn't look that far if the exterior attracted him enough.

"You'll love Segovia," Fabiola said from the back. "It's my favourite place. Queen Isabella the Catholic was proclaimed Queen there in 1474. I expect it was her favourite place too, don't you? She lived in the *alcázar* there whenever she could. She and Ferdinand slept in a very narrow bed for two people. Do you want to see it, Hudi?"

"Will there be time?" Judi asked.

"Probably not today," Don Joaquin answered her. "I have an appointment before lunch which will give you two girls time to look at the Roman Aqueduct. I thought we'd lunch at the Mesón del Duque. You know where it is, Fabiola. See that you and Hudi are there by two-thirty."

"*Sí,* Papa."

His eyes rested lightly on Judi's face. "All right with you, *bombón?*"

Fabiola giggled. "Shall I call you that too, Hudi? You are sweet like a sweetie!"

"What nonsense!" Judi retorted fiercely.

"Well, I like you anyway," Fabiola assured her. "Papa must too, or he wouldn't tease you. He'll tease you all the more if you show him you care. He always does!"

"I don't care!" Judi felt moved to protest. "I think it a silly name, that's all."

Don Joaquin took his hand off the wheel and briefly covered hers with it in an intimate gesture that made her flesh burn.

"Would you prefer *favorita, or preciosa?*"

Judi sighed. "I'll settle for Hudi."

Fabiola gave this her full approval. "It would be Hudi in Spanish," she explained earnestly. "Judi doesn't sound right to me. You see, when I saw it written down in your letter to Abuela, I thought you would pronounce it Hudi, too. Hudi is a pretty name!"

"Isn't Judi?"

"It doesn't sound right," Fabiola dismissed it firmly.

"You'll never win with my daughter, *bombón.* She's an Arnalte through and through!"

She'd never win with any of them! "Y Pizzaro," she mused aloud.

"That's not my name," Fabiola contradicted her. "I'm Fabiola Arnalte y Zamarrala. You're thinking of Papa."

"So I am," Judi acknowledged. "I'm glad I'm just Judi Duggan," she added provocatively.

"Why?" asked Fabiola.

Judi, finding herself faced by two pairs of identical, laughing eyes, turned away from both the father and the daughter with a shrug of her shoulders. "I just am," she said. She was glad to see Segovia in the distance and pointed it out eagerly. "Where's the aqueduct?" she asked. "I thought it went right across the top of the town? It does in the pictures."

"It goes across the main street," Don Joaquin told her. "You'll see it in a minute."

It was an unbelievable sight when she did see it. The ancient stones were raised in arches over the wide street that took up most of the valley between the sloping side streets of the city.

"Shall I let you out here?" Don Joaquin suggested, pausing beside the arches. "Don't forget, Fabiola, two-thirty, or I'll eat lunch without you."

"*Sí*, Papa."

It was cold outside the car. Judi hunched her shoulders into her jacket and stared up at the aqueduct over her head. It towered above her.

"How high is it?" she wondered.

"Twenty-eight-and-a-half metres down here. It's very long though. Seven-hundred-and-twenty-eight metres long. It still brings water from the *Rive* Acebeda into the city."

Judi smiled down at the child. "You seem to know a lot about it."

"I do. Mama came from Segovia. Zamarrala, her village, is only a few kilometres away."

Fabiola eagerly led the way up the hill to display the whole length of the aqueduct to Judi's marvelling eyes. "Trajan built it," she said. "He was a Roman Emperor, but he was really a Spaniard." She gave Judi a naughty look. "Britain wasn't civilised in those days, was it?"

Judi laughed, undismayed. "You shouldn't believe the propaganda of the victors. We only have the Roman's word for it as to what we were like. We may have been more civilised than they were, in fact."

"With roads and things? And aqueducts?"

"With a free people who didn't keep slaves to build such things for them," Judi maintained stoutly.

Fabiola was unimpressed. "I think it's a matter of climate," she said. "You were too busy keeping warm."

Judi was amused by the idea, especially as they rounded the corner at that moment and were caught by a gust of wind that froze them both to the marrow.

"Let's go and look at the shops," Judi suggested. "I thought I might make you a dress for Christmas and you can show me the sort of thing you would like."

Fabiola's face shone with excitement. "A long dress?"

"A short one might be more practical. We'll see."

"Abuela would let you come with me to buy some short dresses, but a long dress would be really special. I could wear it for our Christmas family dance. If you make it big enough, I could wear it for simply *ages!*"

They spent a long time looking in the shop windows. Fabiola had quite an eye for fashion, Judi discovered and, once again, she found herself wondering about the woman who had been her mother. Had the dead Teresa shared the natural flair for style in her dress that was such a feature of the Spaniard, but which, unfortunately, was not shared by Doña Maria, who managed to look like a rag-bag on all and every occasion?

In the end they had to run up the hill to the restaurant where Don Joaquin was waiting for them.

"Only five minutes late," he greeted them wryly.

"We're not late," Judi protested, consulting her watch.

He grinned at her. "For a woman in Spain you could be said to be early. As a nation we have absolutely no sense of time."

"Well I have. What's more, I'm hungry!"

"Then come and eat," he invited her.

It was like stepping into another world as they went inside. Warm, spicy air met them, redolent of the prepared cold meats for which the restaurant was justly famous. The building was medieval and looked it, with its low beams and panelled walls. Some men sat drinking at small tables on one side. The other was completely taken up by a huge glass counter on which was laid out every kind of meat and sausage that one could imagine. Behind the counter stood the proprietor, white-coated and with a chef's hat, and round his neck a sash proclaiming that he was a *Maestro Asador de Segovia,* Master of the Roasts, a title of which he was evidently very proud. Whole hams hung from the ceiling, vying for attention with strings of pimentoes and garlic and the beautiful tiles set in the wall behind the counter.

Judi gasped with pleasure, more hungry than ever. She sniffed appreciatively at the many smells that wafted towards her.

"What a marvellous place!" she exclaimed.

"It's typically Castilian," Don Joaquin told her, pleased by her reaction. "The restaurant is upstairs."

She followed him up the narrow stairs with

Fabiola bringing up the rear, and was just as pleased with what she found up there. The beams were decorated like leather worked in the Arab manner, and the walls were plain, though tiles had been painted onto the lower areas to deceive the eye. The decorations were many and varied, ranging from framed notes of money from all over the world to the signatures of some of the famous people who had sampled the wares of the restaurant.

There were a number of tables, all covered with scarlet cloths, topped by snowy-white ones which could be quickly removed and replaced between sittings. Don Joaquin led the way to the one in the far corner, seating himself beside Judi with Fabiola opposite. A waiter leaped to attention, bending solicitously over them to take their order.

Judi was not surprised when she was not consulted about the menu. Another time, she would have protested vigorously but, for this time, she was quite prepared to leave the whole meal in Don Joaquin's capable hands. She felt warm and comfortable. For the first time since that last, awful meeting with David, she found she could think of him with something like complacency as someone she had once known and liked a little, but had lost touch with long ago.

She smiled to herself. Even the close proximity of Don Joaquin was failing to disturb her as it usually did.

"Wine, *bombón*?"

"I don't know," she confessed. "I'm not accustomed to having wine at lunchtime."

He poured her a glass of wine and one for himself. "It'll help you relax," he said, unperturbed. "Try a little."

She took a sip, not liking to refuse. It tasted very good to her and she realised he had chosen it with care to please her. Some sign of gratitude was obviously called for, but she sat frozen to the seat of her chair, unable to find any words at all. She lowered her lashes, staring at the glass of wine in her hand, willing herself to murmur a light thank you—anything that would divert his attention from herself and her exaggerated reaction to what, in all conscience, had been a simple enough question, even if it had included the pet name he had found for her and which she knew to be quite unsuitable, considering that she was no more than an employee of sorts.

"What about Fabiola?" she said at last.

"She may have some, mixed with a little water." He poured a little in a glass for his daughter, before turning his whole attention back to Judi. "Do you approve of my choice?"

Judi managed a slight nod of her head. "I don't know enough about it to give you much of an opinion," she said. "Is it a local wine?"

"Made with someone like you in mind," he responded promptly. She caught the glint in his eyes and hastily looked away. He raised his glass to her. "*Salud!*"

"*Salud,*" she answered shakily.

A selection of cold meats was put down in front of her and she helped herself from the basket of freshly baked bread in the centre of the table. She was glad to have something to do, some reason for turning her mind away from that glimpse of warm desire she had seen in the depths of his dark eyes. It was flattering, of course, that such a man should find her attractive, but the trouble was that she was attracted, too. If she wasn't very careful she would lose her head and her heart in that order and she was wise enough to know he would never be serious about someone like her, someone of no particular family and a foreigner to boot.

Their plates were cleared away and she still hadn't thought of any suitable topic of conversation with which to amuse him. Fabiola was unnaturally quiet too, occasionally looking at Judi with unabashed curiosity, as if she could feel her discomfiture and was wondering as to its cause.

Judi cleared her throat. "Tell me more about Segovia," she bade the girl. "Tell me about this restaurant."

Fabiola waited for her father to speak, sipping her wine with relish. "You tell her, Papa," she urged him.

He watched the colour come and go in Judi's cheeks, refilling her glass with a generous hand.

"Your King Charles I was here," he obediently began. "He was the Prince of Wales then, and I think he came in search of a bride. That may have been the origin of your nursery rhyme of the silver nutmeg and the golden pear, but I have no proof of that. Like all your countrymen, he thoroughly enjoyed himself in Spain. We turned him into an art collector of some note. I wonder what we'll turn you into?"

"A frog, I expect," she said with some asperity.

"A Spanish Grandee?" Fabiola suggested, entering into the game with enthusiasm.

"No, never that! I'm very happy as I am!" Judi claimed.

"Sometimes," the child remarked, "you look quite sad and not at all happy. Do you want to go back to England?"

"Not yet," Judi admitted.

"Then you must like Spain very much," Fabiola reasoned. "I hope you stay for a long, long time!"

Judi was saved from having to answer by the arrival of their second course. She had never eaten roasted suckling pig before and she was quite sure she shouldn't drink any more of the wine Don Joaquin was plying her with, filling her glass quite as often as he filled his own.

"It would be nice," Fabiola went on when she could, "if you could visit Zamarrala on the feast day of Santa Agueda. That's a very special day when a woman takes command of the village for the whole day. She wears a skirt of blue or claret with silver stripes and velvet fringes. She looks very grand—like a real mayor. She presides over all the religious ceremonies that day, too. Me, I should like that very much. I like to give orders and have people do everything I say. Mama used to say it was a wretched superstition, but I think it would be the greatest fun!"

"I don't think I would enjoy it very much," Judi said with decision. "People hardly ever do as I tell them!"

Fabiola chuckled, putting her head on one side and considering the matter. "Whole armies wouldn't obey you, but some people would. You always ask so nicely, not like some people. Some people think one has nothing better to do than to fetch and carry for them all day long! Tía Leonor—"

Judi shook her head at her and the girl shut up like a trap.

"What about Tía Leonor?" Don Joaquin asked without apparent interest.

Fabiola was only too ready to tell him. "She never wants to do anything interesting," she complained. "All she does is wave a fan in the air and pose for photographs. She couldn't make her own clothes, as Hudi does."

Don Joaquin's lazy eyes went from Fabiola's eager to Judi's embarrassed face. "Do you make your own clothes?"

"Most of them," she admitted. "I knit, too," she added for good measure.

His glance travelled over her with renewed interest. "Very nice, too. Leonor has never had to earn her own living, but she usually manages to get herself noticed."

With that orange hair she could scarcely help it. "It must take quite a lot of doing to keep the castle running smoothly," she offered by way of recompense for the involuntary thought.

"Would you find it beyond you?" he asked her.

"Not once I knew what I was doing," she said, quite sure in her own mind that she could do it on her head with all the servants that there were on hand.

"Yes, you'd be a good peacemaker," he remarked. "For your interest, Leonor has nothing to do with the running of the castle. My mother will never relinquish the task to anyone other than my wife."

"She's asked Leonor to oversee the progress of the chapel," Judi couldn't resist telling him.

"That's my affair. Bring your plans to me, Hudi, and to no one else. Is that clear?"

"Padre Juan—"

"To me, Hudi. If there's any trouble, send them to talk it over with me. I love my family dearly, but the castle is my responsibility, as is the welfare of everybody in it—including you."

It must have been all the wine that made her quite ready to argue her case with him. She shook her head and pursed up her lips with determination.

"You may be paying me for my professional services, but nobody is responsible for me but myself!"

"You make us sound like strangers," he taunted her.

"So we are!" she declared.

"*Strangers*? I think not, *bombón!*"

"And don't call me by that ridiculous name!" she snapped, knowing that he was remembering that she had hardly behaved like a stranger when he had kissed her that morning.

"I'll call you what I like." He smiled at her. "Is there any real reason why I shouldn't?"

Judi was just considering throwing her glass of wine in his face when Fabiola gave a happy sigh from the other side of the table.

"I'm so glad you brought us today, Papa. It's been such a long time since we've gone out anywhere as a family."

"But I'm not family," Judi put in quickly, wondering why she should be feeling so miserable about it. What was this family to her, after all?

"Not real family," Fabiola agreed, making

Judi feel worse than ever. "But it doesn't matter. I like you much better than a lot of my family—and so does Papa or he wouldn't have brought you with us." She put down her knife and fork with another sigh of content. "I wish we could do this every day!" she added.

Chapter Five

Autumn changed to winter. The winds grew colder and the trees shed the last of their leaves. Occasional flurries of snow left their traces on the view from her window, but were seldom to be met with on her trips into the small town behind the castle. Christmas was coming and Judi began to think about going home to her parents for the holiday. She made no arrangements, though, almost as if she were waiting to be persuaded to stay in Spain and celebrate Christmas with her employers. It was a matter she put out of her mind whenever it occurred to her, which was unlike her, because she usually liked to have her plans pretty cut and dried.

It had been three weeks of hard work. She had shut herself away from the family, concentrating hard on her designs, the materials she wanted to use and finding the right people to help her

to make and embroider the first set of vestments
and altar cloths that would be used for the first
time on Christmas Day. Doña Maria had been
unexpectedly helpful here, finding a small con-
vent of nuns who earned their living with their
needles and were more than content to work
under Judi's general direction.

Since that first morning, Judi had had her
breakfast in her room like the rest of the family.
She told herself that she wasted less time that
way in getting the day's work started, but every
day it remained a temptation to her to change
her mind and have breakfast with Don Joaquin
downstairs. Of course, it was likely that he was
no longer using the glassed-in verandah now
that it was so much colder. Perhaps he was even
having his breakfast in his room also. It was a
dreary thought.

On the morning before Christmas Eve she
realised they were not going to have enough gold
and silver thread to complete the embroidery on
the stoll. She would go out herself, she decided,
and hope to find some of the precious thread in
one of the local shops. She enjoyed her visits to
the town with its narrow, cobbled streets. She
particularly liked the shops, the *bodegas*, which
sold local wines and brandies loose and which
smelt like the inside of a wine-barrel themselves, the delicatessen which sold something of
everything in the way of food and the greengro-
cers whose products still depended on the time
of year and not on exotic imports from abroad.

The streets were gay with the decorations for
the coming festival. The camel on which one of
the Three Kings was to ride on Epiphany was
already installed in a nearby stable to the end-

less fascination of the children. The costumes were ready, as Judi very well knew, for the maids at the castle had soon enlisted her aid in their preparation. She had been amused to discover that the meetings that went on to get everything together were very much the same as the ones she had attended back in England.

Today there was an added air of expectancy in the streets. Judi had put on her warmest coat and was still managing to feel cold, when she was summoned urgently into a small house she was passing.

"Señorita, we are having an argument and I was just saying that for sure *La Inglesa* would know the answer! Come in, come in!"

Judi paused outside the house. If she went inside she knew she would not come out before lunchtime.

"Buenos días, señora. I am in a hurry before the shops shut—"

"This'll take but a moment, Señorita Hudi. Should we ask Doña Maria, the Señorita Leonor or yourself to present the gifts at the feast of the Three Kings?"

Judi was taken aback by the question. "What usually happens?" she asked.

"Last year it was Doña Maria who stepped in for her daughter-in-law. The poor thing died shortly before Christmas as you know, but Don Joaquin didn't want the children to be disappointed. He is very good that way."

"Then I should ask Doña Maria again this year," Judi suggested.

The Spanish woman gave her a sly look. "It's rumoured that Don Joaquin will be marrying again. The little one needs a mother."

"He'll hardly be married by January sixth!" Judi exclaimed.

"But we don't wish to slight his *novia*. Doña Teresa did a lot for our town and we're hoping the next one will do the same."

Judi felt a bleak space in her middle. If it was all about town that Don Joaquin was marrying again it must be true. He must have decided that Leonor would suit him after all.

"I still think Doña Maria is the one to ask," she said aloud. "If Don Joaquin has a fiancée by then, she'll doubtless tell you, don't you think?"

"If you say so, señorita. I've heard it said we'll all be surprised by his choice. Have you heard this?"

"I haven't heard anything at all," Judi said shortly. How could he want to marry Leonor? She would make him perfectly miserable and, worse, Fabiola didn't like her.

"Ah, well, we mustn't keep you," the señora said pleasantly. "Stop by on your way back if you have time. There's always a cup of coffee for you here. *La Inglesa* has earned her place in our town. There's not one of us would turn you away!"

Judi was touched. "I'm beginning to think of it as my town," she confided. "You all make me so welcome here."

She hurried on her way without a backward look. The wind in her face stung her eyes, making them water. *Leonor!* Why did it have to be her? All right, so she was suitable, coming from the right family and having all the right connections, but what did she have to offer Don Joaquin as a woman? Judi conjured up a vision of the Spanish girl in her mind's eye and felt more depressed than ever. Leonor had a beauty all her own. She was distinctive and exciting. It wouldn't be so surprising if that was the kind of woman Don Joaquin wanted. He'd been satiated with niceness the last time round and, there was no doubt about it, Leonor wasn't *nice* at all!

She rounded the corner to where the traffic policeman stood on a small stand in the middle of the town square and directed the traffic. He was a rotund, though popular figure, blowing his whistle madly and shaking an irate finger as his charges tried to slip past him when he wasn't looking. Today, his grin was as broad as his face, as the town's citizens wished him the compliments of the season, leaving their gifts in a steadily growing pile at his feet.

Judi stood and watched him for a moment, wondering what would happen if he had to move off his stand in an emergency. The piles of bottles of drink and food hampers were already up to his waist. Soon he wouldn't be able to see over the tops of them!

Quite suddenly, she wanted to join in the fun. She went into the *bodega* at the corner of the square and asked for the only kind of wine she knew, the one Don Joaquin had ordered in Segovia, coming out with it triumphantly under one arm.

The policeman saw her approaching and wished her a Happy Christmas.

"Happy Christmas!" she called back to him and, with due ceremony, deposited the bottle on the still growing pile. She would have liked to see the Traffic Wardens attracting a like pile of goodies back home in England!

"Hey, señorita, wait a moment!"

She laughed up at him. "That's for seeing me safely across the square so often!" she told him.

"*Gracias, pero—*"

She took to her heels and ran, not wanting his thanks. Once a Spaniard got started on a formal speech of thanks, it could go on for hours, and she didn't think she really deserved any thanks at all. It was more for her pleasure than for his that she had bought the wine.

A silence fell over the small group of black-clad women in the needlework shop as she entered. She smiled impersonally at them all, trying not to be aware that they had been talking about her and were embarrassed by her sudden appearance.

"*Feliz Navidad!*" she murmured shyly.

The bubble of silence broke as they all returned her greeting, each eager to outdo the other. She was obviously in a hurry, they observed, and if she wanted to be served before them, not one of them would mind in the least. On the contrary, it would be a pleasure to wait while she made her purchases. Would the chapel be ready in time for the great feast? Was Padre Juan pleased with her efforts?

Judi answered all their questions, relaxing a little. If they had been talking about her she felt it would have been kindly. The more she mixed with these Castilian women, the more she liked and admired them. They lived hard lives, many of them without much comfort, yet they displayed a humour and a love for their families that never seemed to flag. A joke was more effective than a complaint and, if it had an earthy flavour, so much the better. They knew what the earth was, worked it with their own hands and bent backs, and still found time to dress up and dance all night at every fiesta that came along.

Judi made her purchases in a happier frame of mind, thankful to find the shopkeeper had had the foresight to buy extra quantities of everything he thought she might need.

"I was afraid you wouldn't have any gold or silver thread," she confessed to him.

"And have you go all the way to Madrid, señorita? Your order is very valuable to us. You have only to ask for what you need and we'll get it in for you—always!"

She wondered if she should warn him not to get carried away in his hopes for future orders. Once she had finished at the *alcázar* she would be going back to England, and she couldn't imagine Leonor buying much locally, not even the smallest household goods.

That night, she worked into the small hours of the morning to finish the stole. Fabiola's dress had taken up a lot of her spare time recently and she felt guilty about leaving so much of the manual work to the nuns, glad as they were of the work. She was accustomed to seeing her own work through from beginning to end, designing them, working them, and embroidering them herself and, although this was the largest task she had ever tackled, she felt she was cheating by having half the work done for her.

In the morning she overslept. A sharp rap at her door jerked her out of sleep and into a reality she preferred not to face just then. For a few blissful hours she had been able to forget that Don Joaquin was marrying Leonor as soon as he came out of mourning, but now, again, the knowledge sat on her shoulders like an evil sprite, mocking her with the echoes of her own hopes, which she had had no right to entertain for a moment, but which had somehow managed to become a part of her, without conscious thought.

Fabiola's head came round the door. "Hudi, Hudi, what are you doing? Abuela and Tía Leonor say the police are here! Papa has them in the salon, but it's *you* they've come to see! What have you done? They all look very grave! Have you murdered someone?"

"Not that I know about," Judi responded grumpily.

"Not yet?" Fabiola teased her. "You're looking sad again, and you haven't looked sad for ages!"

Judi tried to summon up a smile. "I can't think what the Guarda Civil should want with me," she said.

"It couldn't be murder," Fabiola laughed at her. "It's the traffic police who want you. Have you stolen someone's car?"

"Not recently."

"But could you?" the child persisted. "I mean, could you drive Papa's car if you wanted to?"

"In England I could. I'd need an International licence to drive in Spain and I didn't bother to get one because I didn't think I'd need it."

"Then you must have walked against a red light!"

Judi laughed reluctantly with her. She pulled

herself out of bed and put on the first clothes
that came to hand, a cream coloured dress with
scarlet knots embroidered round the neckline. It
was one of her favourite dresses because it
brought out the storm-grey of her eyes and com-
plimented the fairness of her hair.

She wasn't sure whether she should knock on
the door of the salon or not. She was just trying
to make up her mind when Don Joaquin turned
his head and saw her.

"Here is Señorita Hudi now," he said to the
two grey-uniformed men with him. They had
their white helmets tucked under their arms
and stood to attention, their feet a little apart,
looking for all the world like Tweedledee and
Tweedledum as they bowed in unison and
wished her good morning.

"Have I done something wrong?" Judi asked
them.

"On the contrary, señorita. A happy feast to
you!"

"And to you!"

They even smiled in unison, their eyes swivel-
ling to Don Joaquin's watchful face. "If the
señor would like to explain. You have nothing to
worry about, señorita, nothing at all! Only, we
believe you visited the town yesterday?"

Judi found herself looking at Don Joaquin too.
"I bought some gold and silver thread," she
explained to him. "I needed it before the shops
shut for Christmas."

By contrast to the policemen, Don Joaquin
was completely at his ease. Judi tried not to
notice how well his clothes fit him, accentuating
his slim-hipped, long-legged male shape, a challenge to her own femininity, making her deeply

aware of the burgeoning needs within herself that he could arouse merely by looking at her.

He put his hand on her arm and she felt a sudden tightness of her flesh. It was unfair that he should have such an effect on her. Unfair and unwise! She stepped away from him, but he only followed, his hand possessive and drawing her closer beside him.

"You left a gift for the police?" he asked her.

So that was what it was all about! Did they only accept presents from the local people?

She nodded. "It was only a bottle of wine."

The policemen smiled approvingly in unison. "The señorita's gift is much appreciated. We have come to thank you. If the señor permits, we have brought a Christmas card for you. We would have sent it through the post, but we know you only as Señorita Hudi from the castle."

"Judi Duggan," Judi supplied in a small voice.

They gave her a united, bewildered look, before turning to Don Joaquin. "*La Inglesa* has an unpronounceable name! How you say this Chudi Duxxan?" They laughed at their efforts. "*La Inglesa* is joking!"

"No, that really is her name," Don Joaquin told them. "My daughter calls her Hudi and we all follow her example—sometimes."

When he didn't embarrass her with ludicrous pet names, Judi thought uncomfortably.

With his uncanny knack of reading her thoughts she was sure he knew what she was thinking. His lips twitched and his hand tightened on her arm before he released her.

"A *copa* of wine before you go?" he suggested to the policemen.

Judi hurried over to a chair that was set against the wall by itself and sat down, isolating herself from the men as she did so. She took a deep breath, annoyed that the only thing that kept her there was that, if she left, Don Joaquin would know she was running away and would draw his own conclusions. If he wanted Leonor, Leonor would have to be enough for him! Judi had no intention of fulfilling the role of passing fancy while he waited for the right moment to marry another woman.

She realised she had made a mistake almost immediately. The policemen were served with a generous measure of wine which they accepted gratefully, sitting down side by side on a small French gilt sofa that looked as if it might collapse at any moment under their weight. Don Joaquin poured two more glasses and brought one over to her. He leaned over the back of her chair in an indolent stance that had her trembling with anticipation lest he should touch her hair or the back of her neck.

"What wine did you give them?" he asked in an undertone.

"The wine we had in Segovia."

"We shall have to expand your knowledge of our wines. What do you think of this one?"

She took a sip, and choked over her glass. He took it from her, putting it down beside her, and patted her firmly on the back. She had always thought that to be the most useless gesture of help to be offered by anyone, but Don Joaquin hit the exact spot and she stopped coughing and recovered herself, feeling more than a little foolish.

"Try again!" he said, returning her glass to

her. The look in his dark eyes were warm and appreciative and she felt a lot less silly.

"It's very nice," she murmured, not really knowing if it was wine or water. If he went on looking at her like that, she wouldn't even know her own name! She would be the anonymous *La Inglesa,* sometimes called Hudi, for the rest of her life. She wouldn't be Judi Duggan at all!

She took another sip and blinked. It was good. She looked up at him through her lashes, meaning to tell him so, but his expression mocked her as he turned away, going back to the policemen and leaving her to her own devices. She watched him as he joined them, immediately taking command of the conversation and putting the two awkward men at their ease. He was confident to the point of arrogance and she envied him that. She would have liked to be able to dismiss him as casually as he did her, amusing herself with him when he was there and forgetting all about him when he was not.

The policemen drained their glasses and stood up to go. They renewed their thanks to her for the bottle of wine, more at home after their *copa,* probably the first of many before they went off duty that evening.

"You are spoken about in the town a great deal," one of them remarked to her. "The *patrón* himself brought you from England, didn't he?"

"Doña Maria—"

They nodded their heads, satisfied. "Of course, Doña Maria! You couldn't have come here without her. How goes Doña Teresa's chapel?"

"We'll be using it for Midnight Mass," Don Joaquin told them. "Señorita Hudi is an expert in designing vestments and altar linen. We were fortunate to obtain her services."

"Such a pretty young lady—"

"I am fully qualified," Judi interrupted firmly. "I have to work for my living, you know."

"*Claro! Las Inglesas* pride themselves on their independence! The *patrón* will be finding more work for you when the chapel is finished! Now you are here, señorita, the family won't want to let you go!"

The Spanish were a gallant people, Judi thought sourly, but she could have done without their compliments just then, with Don Joaquin taking amused note of everything they said to her. Did he think she would let their comments go to her head? Did he think she didn't know he'd already decided to marry Leonor as soon as he could? Did he think she didn't know all about Latin men and how they flirted as easily as they breathed?

The policemen bowed over her hand but made no attempt to kiss it. Judi remembered that Don Joaquin had told her that it wasn't the woman's hand they were kissing at all, but her marriage ring. She hadn't believed him altogether, but now she began to think that it must be so.

"*Adiós*, señorita. *Hasta la vista.*"

"*Adiós*, señores," she responded.

She would have gone with them, escaping to the security of her own rooms, but Don Joaquin was before her, his restraining hand on her shoulder all the time he was saying goodbye to the policemen and tipping them handsomely for their trouble in coming.

"Wait a minute, Hudi, I want to speak to you,"

he said over his shoulder as he went with them to the door.

She considered her chances of slipping past him without his noticing that she had gone, and despised herself for her weakness in wanting to stay. She sat down again and finished her glass of wine with deliberation. She had to speak to him sometime about the next phase in her work for the chapel and it might as well be now.

He stood in front of her for a long moment, looking her over with a fierce concentration that made her pulse race.

"What did you want to speak to me about?" she asked huskily.

"I forget. Whenever I find myself alone with you I forget everything else," he said with unexpected frankness.

Judi was shocked into movement. She put her glass down on the nearest ledge and made a rush for the door. She had to get away from him before she did something unforgivable and forgot all about Leonor and what the Spanish girl was going to mean to him in the near future.

He caught her by the hand and, even while she tried to escape his hold, she couldn't help admiring the speed with which he could move and the way he used his body, getting the maximum of power out of the minimum of effort.

"Don't you feel something of the same?" he whispered to her. "Don't you want to be in my arms and share my kisses?"

She stared at him, refusing to answer, her insides turning to water and her knees to jelly.

"I—I need to get on with my work!" she said at last. His eyes were warm and dark, almost affectionate, and if she stayed a minute longer she would forget all about her pride—

"Have pity, *bombón!* You give of yourself to everyone but me! Haven't you any time for me at all?"

"I didn't come here to be your plaything!"

His anger singed her confidence, making her more pliable as he pulled her into the circle of his arms, kissing the tip of her nose.

"Is this always going to be enough for you, *querida?*"

She gave way to the pressure of his hands, standing so close to him that she could feel his heart beating against her breast.

"*Querida! Bombón!*" she mocked. "What next?"

Her words lit the fuse of his desire for her and his mouth took hers with a fierceness that betrayed his anger. He forced her lips apart and plundered the moistness of her mouth, ignoring her struggles to be free. Nor did she really want to escape from his embrace. Her hands found their way beneath his jacket and made their way over the smooth, hard muscles of his back, and up to the short hairs of the back of his neck.

"Ah, Hudi, I need you so much," he breathed against her mouth. "I want you!"

She wanted him too. She was on a roller coaster of desire that gave her no time to think of anything else but him, the feel of him, the warm male smell of him, and the strength of his arms about her.

"Come closer!" he commanded her.

"Joaquin, *please!*" she whispered.

"I want to make love to you," he responded. "I've wanted you in my bed since the first moment I saw you. What are you that you have this effect on me? Are you a witch or a woman?"

"Kiss me again!" she begged him.

His lips descended on hers once again. She thought she should hide herself away from him; then she thought that it wasn't her fault, she had done nothing to invite him to kiss her; then she didn't think at all, giving way to the needs of her own body as much as to him.

Her fingers undid his shirt, moving over his warm skin, enjoying the slight frisson of the roughness of his hair and the smoothness of his skin.

"Will you let me love you?" he asked her.

It was like surfacing from a very deep dive and finding the sunshine had turned to rain on the water.

"I never have—"

"I want you, *bombón,* and you want me."

"How do you know?" She pushed herself away from him and found herself drowning in the warm depths of his eyes.

"I know. Just as I know that this man of yours in England never made you feel this way. You were never his as you will be mine!"

The naked triumph in his voice restored a little of her sanity. She pulled her clothes back together, not daring to look at him again. "I'm not yours!" she said baldly.

"You will be!"

Her heart knocked against her ribs. She licked her lips in unconscious provocation, giving herself time to think, but just as she was about to answer there was a furious gasp from the doorway.

Leonor advanced into the room, her hips

swinging as if she were up on the catwalk and showing off the impossible dress she was wearing.

"I was looking for you," she said to Judi. "I thought you were serious about your work, not the *patrón*—"

"I only wish that she were more serious about the *patrón*," Don Joaquin interrupted Leonor's angry tirade. His hand tightened over Judi's. "But, alas, I am afraid that she has lost her heart to our chapel—" His tone was dry.

"You men are all the same!" Leonor cried. "And as for you, Judi, don't think your little scheme will work! It's my duty, you know, to tell Doña Maria what you are up to! You will probably find yourself back in England for Christmas whether you like it or not!"

Judi felt that she could take no more. She wrenched her hand free and ran from the room without even a backward glance at Don Joaquin or Leonor.

Chapter Six

Alone in her room, Judi finished embroidering the white stole. She was annoyed to find her hands were still shaking from her encounter with Leonor. How was she ever going to explain to Doña Maria how she had come to be kissing her son in the salon? If it had been a light, flirtatious kiss and nothing more it might have been excusable, but Judi was sure Leonor would take delight in recounting every detail of exactly how she had discovered Don Joaquin, for which Judi was wholly to blame, for it was well known that men only took what was offered to them.

The expected summons downstairs to Doña Maria's private sitting-room never came. Judi ate a solitary lunch in the middle of the afternoon and, for the first time since coming to Spain, felt thoroughly lonely and unsettled. She wished she had gone back to England for the festival. At least her parents wouldn't have left her on her own all day. Christmas Eve was always a busy day at home, with all the last preparations to be done, the wrapping of parcels and the decorating of the tree. Here, everyone else was busy, but she had no preparations to make and very little work she could do now that the white vestments were complete and ready for use.

She was just putting her lunch things back on the tray when there was a knock at her door, followed immediately by Fabiola's normal, impetuous entry.

"Abuela is coming!" the girl announced.

Judi cringed inwardly. "Coming up here?"

Fabiola beamed at her. "She's coming to see my dress! You see, I've *almost* persuaded her that I can wear it at Mass tonight, as well as at the party tomorrow. She thinks, though, you might want to wrap it up and have me wait until after Mass to undo it. I told her you wouldn't be mean enough for that! You won't be, will you, Hudi?"

"You can have it now if you like," Judi told her.

She went through the bathroom into her bedroom and took the dress from her wardrobe and laid it on the bed. It was one of the best things she had ever done, she thought. It had been made with real love for Fabiola and it showed.

"Is that it?" Fabiola demanded, following her more slowly. "It's beautiful! The most beautiful dress I've ever seen!"

"I'm glad you like it," Judi responded more soberly. "Though I think almost anything would look good on you."

"*Sí*, I'm Spanish," the girl acknowledged with a little shrug. "Almost anything, but not those silly velvet dresses that have no style at all! I wish Mama could have seen me in this!"

"Was your mother interested in clothes?" This was a new insight on the dead Teresa and, to Judi, a wholly unexpected one.

Fabiola gave her an impish smile. "She was Spanish, too," she said simply. "Only Abuela doesn't like to talk about clothes. Papa says it's because she has Portuguese blood as well as Spanish. He says the Portuguese aren't nearly so smart as the Spanish!"

Judi laughed. They were still laughing together when Doña Maria appeared in the doorway.

"Fabiola," she rebuked her granddaughter, "you're not to make a nuisance of yourself. You must learn to wait until something is offered to you, not demand it as of right."

"*Sí*, Abuela." Judi smiled at the meek tones and was rewarded by a conspiratorial grimace. "Hudi *wants* me to wear the dress tonight!" she added in her more usual, forthright manner.

Doña Maria came further into the room. "Is that the dress?" she asked, and she appeared suddenly nervous.

"Do you like it?" Judi asked her.

"My dear, you've achieved the impossible! How I wish Teresa were here to see her daughter in that! Put it on, *niña*, and let's see if you do it justice. I hope you've thanked Hudi properly for it?"

Fabiola grinned widely. "I knew you'd call her Hudi in the end," she teased her grandmother. "She doesn't seem like *La Inglesa* any longer, does she?"

Doña Maria was embarrassed, but she hid it well. "I suppose she doesn't. I never thought an English woman could come to be one of us, but Hudi has come as near to it as possible. We'll miss her when she goes home, won't we, Fabiola?"

Fabiola was busy getting out of her ill-fitting, despised velvet dress. "I'd prefer it if some other person went," she muttered. "We wouldn't miss *her* at all!"

Oh, how much Judi wished that, too! Even Doña Maria looked resigned rather than enthusiastic as she said, "You're too young to understand, *pequeña,* but your father has need of a wife. He can't mourn your mother forever. If he chooses to marry Leonor, we must accept his choice. Do you understand me?"

"*Sí,* Abuela."

Doña Maria sighed gustily. "Let's hope this time he will have a woman who'll put him first. His father and I were overanxious about his first marriage and maybe we overpersuaded him that Teresa was right for him," she confided in an undertone to Judi, frowning at Fabiola as if this would, somehow, prevent the child from hearing what she was saying. "Of course, someone in his position must make a suitable marriage. *Claro!* Ah well, perhaps Leonor will be a comfort to him."

Judi couldn't imagine Leonor being a comfort to anyone, but she could hardly say as much and, anyway, she felt too miserable to care. If she had needed any confirmation that Don Joaquin was about to announce his engagement to the Spanish girl, Doña Maria had confirmed her worst fears. If anyone knew about her son's plans it would be she. What a dreadful Christmas this was turning out to be!

Fabiola put the natural coloured, heavy wild-silk dress over her head, caressing with gentle fingers the scarlet embroidered heraldic nut-megs and pears. She turned immediately to Judi for her to do her up at the back.

"Do I look nice, Hudi? Will Papa be pleased?"

"You look like a fairy-tale princess," Judi assured her.

"In a fairy-tale castle!" Fabiola approved. "But the princess who lives happily ever after is the one who marries the prince who owns the castle. Tía Leonor doesn't make much of a princess—only, I'm afraid Papa might think she does."

"Never mind, you'll be your father's princess tonight," Judi replied warmly. She couldn't see Leonor as a princess either. She would be much better cast as witch, or ugly sister.

It took all of Doña Maria's authority to persuade Fabiola to take off her new dress and to go and lie down for a while as she would be up for the greater part of the night.

If Judi had been wise, she would have followed the same prescription. Instead, she worried about her own clothes and had tried on just about everything she possessed before it was finally time to go down and join the family for the evening.

Fish was served that night. It was plainly cooked with a minimum of trouble taken over it by the cook.

"I expect that's why Papa's gone out to dinner," Fabiola said, pushing her unappetising portion about her plate as though she hoped, by some miracle, that that would make it disappear.

She didn't say that Leonor was missing, too. Judi had caught a glimpse of her as she had come down the stairs, dressed from head to foot in black in a dress so daring that she had wondered how she could possibly wear it. It had a see-through top and nothing underneath, and its most modest feature was its neckline with its neat Peter Pan collar. Ignoring Judi, she threw a shocking-pink cape about her shoulders. The effect was startlingly dramatic against her orange hair. No wonder Don Joaquin was fascinated by her, Judi thought dismally. He probably didn't care that, apart from her appearance, she would hold no surprises for anyone. Perhaps Spaniards didn't mind being bored out of their minds by their wives as long as they were satisfactory in other ways. She refused to allow herself to think about these other ways.

The pause between dinner and Midnight Mass was an uncomfortable one. Fabiola looked longingly at the array of parcels stacked neatly beneath the tree and, at intervals, wondered aloud where her father had got to. Judi had other worries of her own. She had chosen an Empire-style gown in the end and had dressed her curly hair into a windswept style that she had thought looked good on her. But, although she had expected everyone to dress up for the occasion, she had been startled to see Doña Maria in the full dress of her people, her hair dressed with comb and mantilla, and with an obviously very valuable fan in her hand.

"Have you no mantilla to cover your head?"

Fabiola asked her as they made a move towards the chapel.

"No," Judi answered her shortly. She felt plain and ordinary and the vision Leonor had presented was still in her mind's eye.

"It doesn't matter," Fabiola assured her. "Abuela looks nice tonight, doesn't she?"

Judi agreed that she did, but she was really wondering if Leonor would come into the chapel without a change of clothes. Probably she would, and carry off the event as if it were quite normal for people to go to church half-naked!

The chapel looked beautiful. Great bowls of holly disguised much of the bare concrete, and the skillful simplicity of Judi's designs for the altar and vestments were as lovely as she had hoped they would be. Yet she felt no triumph at all. She was as miserable as she had been all day and Doña Maria's whispered compliments passed her by unheeded.

She sat on the other side of the chapel from where the family sat, searching for her place in the missal because the Spanish responses were still unfamiliar to her. Padre Juan paused in the doorway of the vestry, his vestments shimmering. The altar boy turned on the newly rigged lights. In the sudden burst of light, Judi didn't notice that someone had come to sit beside her.

"Muy guapa!" Don Joaquin said in her ear.

"I'm glad you're pleased," she answered distantly.

"Beautiful and modest, *bombón*. What a pity we're not alone!"

"I prefer things as they are!"

"I have to speak with you, Hudi," he said more

urgently. "It was a pity I had to go out this evening—"

"I'm sure you had a good time!"

He leaned towards her, looking deep into her storm-grey eyes. "Will you breakfast with me tomorrow morning?"

"Certainly not!"

"But I *must* speak with you—"

"Hush!" she said harshly. "I came to pray, not to argue with you!"

His lips twitched and her heart began to thud against her ribs. He really was the most exciting man she had ever met—or was ever likely to! She lowered her eyes to her missal, and all the time a little voice in her head began to throb its message that Leonor hadn't come into the chapel with him. Was it possible she had not been out with him at all?

"If you don't come to me, I'll come to you," he threatened softly. "Shall I join you in your room for breakfast?"

And what would the family make of that? Judi scorned to answer him. She felt him stiffen by her side and eyed him covertly through her lashes, but he was not looking at her. His gaze was on his daughter and the delight in his eyes gave her a painful pleasure. She wondered if Fabiola looked very like her mother, and if he would ever look at her in that way. She caught herself up with a slight sniff. Why should he? She would never mean anything more than a passing incident in his life.

"We have much to thank you for, *bombón,* my daughter most of all. You've made her beautiful tonight!"

They knelt for the canon. With determination,

Judi gave her whole mind to what Padre Juan was saying and, almost before she was aware, she was taking her place at the altar-rails for communion.

Fabiola tugged at her father's hand, nudging his attention in Judi's direction.

"See!" she hissed. "I told you!"

Judi could feel herself blushing beneath the hard look from his dark eyes. What fancy had Fabiola taken into her head now? Was there something wrong with her dress? Should she have worn something over her head after all?

One look from Doña Maria reduced everyone to silence. They returned to their places, their long skirts swishing round their feet. Doña Maria spread her fan with a flick of the fingers of one hand and closed it again with a snap. It was a signal for them all to rise and make their way to the salon below to open their presents. Judi made her way towards the Spanish woman.

"Will you excuse me if I go back to my room?" she murmured to her.

Doña Maria poked her impatiently with the fan. "Nonsense, child! Fabiola would never forgive you if you disappeared now! Her father is pleased with the dress?"

"I think so," Judi said shyly.

"I thought that was what he was whispering to you about."

"He—he did," Judi admitted with a heightened colour. She raised her chin proudly, refusing to take any responsibility for anything that Don Joaquin might do. "He'd do better to tell Fabiola how nice she's looking!" she added with some asperity.

"So," Doña Maria pursued her quarry, "he had something else to say as well?"

"He wanted to speak to me—about the chapel, I expect."

Doña Maria clicked her tongue against her teeth in disapproval. "He ought to know better at his age! Couldn't he have spoken to you about the chapel at some other time?"

"I intend to, Mama," Don Joaquin cut her off with a smile. "I've already asked Hudi to breakfast with me tomorrow morning."

Doña Maria swallowed noisily. "On Christmas Day?"

He shrugged. "Why not? I shall enjoy her company!"

Judi turned to him, an angry warning in her eyes. "I shall sleep late tomorrow," she informed him. "I shall sleep until lunchtime!"

He looked straight back at her. "Nine o'clock. If you're not there, I'll bring a tray up for you—"

"I keep my door locked!"

He put out a hand, pushing a lock of hair off her forehead. "That won't stop me, *mi amor*. You should know that by now."

Judi closed her eyes, feeling as though her insides didn't quite belong to her. When she opened them again, Fabiola had distracted her grandmother's attention and Don Joaquin was offering her his arm, a knowing smile on his face, just as if he knew how badly she wanted to give in to his wishes. *But she wasn't going to do it!* She couldn't afford to be alone with him again—

"I have to talk to you, Hudi," he said very gently. "We'll both regret it if I don't. Please, pretty *bombón*, do as I ask—just this once."

Just this once? That was a laugh! She couldn't trust herself to be alone with him for five seconds without the power of his attraction overwhelming her. Five seconds and she would be putty in his hands. Five seconds more and she would forget all about Leonor, all about everything but her own need for him.

"I can't," she gasped out.

"Nine o'clock," he repeated more sternly.

He released her hand as they entered the salon, going straight to his daughter's side. Judi stood where he had left her, trying to control her trembling as she rubbed the place where his fingers had brushed against her skin. It wasn't fair that he could do this to her, crushing her pride and exposing her vulnerability for all to see. She had no business to think of him as a man at all. He was her *employer*, nothing more. She would go back to England and forget all about him! She knew she would never be able to forget the power Don Joaquin had over her emotions. All other men would be compared to him and found wanting. By comparison David had meant nothing to her at all, a mere something to be shrugged off as a shadow disappears in full light. But Joaquin—he would be disturbing her dreams when she was old and grey, and she hated him for it!

She shook her head. "I can't," she repeated.

He bent his head till they were almost touching. "Wait and see!" he said.

"Should we wait for Tía Leonor?" Fabiola demanded, moving closer and closer to the tree and her presents.

"Not if you don't want to," her father laughed at her. "Will you hand them out?"

Fabiola took the task seriously. There was one parcel in particular she was longing to take from under the tree, but she moved it to one side, casting a quick look at her grandmother to see if she approved as she did so. She found a package for Doña Maria to open, one for her father, and one for herself. Then she returned to the first parcel, taking it to Doña Maria with a conspiratorial laugh.

"It's for you, Señorita Hudi," the Spanish woman explained. She rose from her seat, delivering it personally into Judi's hands. "It is from all of us. I hope you will find a good use for it."

Judi hadn't expected to receive anything from them. As well as the dress for Fabiola, she had embroidered her grandmother some handkerchieves, but she had baulked at getting anything for Don Joaquin or for Leonor. She hadn't wanted to give anything to the latter, and she had told herself that Don Joaquin would have been embarrassed to have had a gift from her.

Yet she couldn't stop herself from seeking him out now with her eyes, searching his face to see if he had known about this present for her. It was obvious that he had, that he might even have chosen it himself. In that instant, she knew she had fallen head over heels in love with him. It was no passing attraction she felt for him; it was a strong, irrevocable emotion that had taken possession of her heart and mind.

She undid the knot in the string, smiling at Fabiola dancing her impatience at this added delay.

"You won't need the paper again, Hudi. Tear it off!"

"No, I won't. It's the prettiest paper I've ever seen. Why shouldn't I keep it?"

"Hurry up! Shall I help you?"

"Open one of your own!" Judi told her.

"But I want to see your face when you see what it is!" Her fingers pulled at the edge of the paper, revealing a corner of a small box in Toledo steel, black and inlaid with gold. "It's very old!" Fabiola told her eagerly. "It comes from the time of the Catholic Kings. Perhaps Queen Isabella actually used it herself!"

Judi opened the box and found it had been completely fitted out as a needlecase, complete with its original needles and pins, ivory bobbins for the different coloured threads and a pair of very old scissors, also fashioned in the famous Toledo damascene work which had been brought to Spain by the Arabs.

"Are you sure you want me to have it?" she burst out. "It must be a family heirloom at least!"

She addressed the question to Don Joaquin, but it was Doña Maria who answered: "It's of small consequence compared with all the work you put in on Fabiola's dress, my dear. Don't disappoint her by refusing us the pleasure of giving you something we know you'll value in return."

"I chose it!" Fabiola said proudly.

Doña Maria frowned at her. "I seem to remember your Papa had something to do with it, and I, myself, spent a long time tidying it up because you were too impatient to sort out all the different colours."

"It's true," Fabiola admitted. "But when Papa

suggested it, I was the one who said it was exactly what you'd like!"

Don Joaquin had suggested it? Judi bent her head and traced the intricate pattern on the box with her finger.

"Do you like it?" Fabiola insisted.

Judi hugged her tight. "I love it!" she said.

"Well, well," said Leonor, entering the salon and pausing dramatically, "what a touching little scene! I see you didn't think to wait for me."

"It's long past Fabiola's bedtime," Doña Maria began comfortably.

"And she doesn't care if I get any presents or not," Leonor said in taut tones, glaring at Judi. "It's time she learned she can't always have everything she wants. Send her to bed by all means! We won't miss her, or the señorita, either!"

Fabiola's face became totally expressionless. "Did you have a good evening, Tía Leonor?" she asked politely.

"No, I didn't! Your father seemed to think you couldn't celebrate the Christmas Mass without him." Leonor came forward and put a possessive hand on Don Joaquin's arm, her whole manner changing to one of seduction as she smiled up at him, pouting prettily. "You know I hate having to come home on my own, *querido*. You could have waited a little longer!"

"I thought Stefano would bring you back with him."

"Stefano isn't you!"

Don Joaquin, apparently without moving at all, freed himself of her restraining hand, picking up a small package from beneath the tree as he did so.

"Your present, Leonor. Happy Christmas, my dear."

Leonor snatched it open and held up the elaborate string of pearls she found within. "Teresa's pearls! I've always envied her them! Why aren't you keeping them for Fabiola? I suppose you want to keep them in the family?"

"I am family!" Fabiola cried out.

"For now," Leonor murmured, fastening the double rope about her neck and preening herself happily.

Fabiola stamped her foot, as thoroughly enraged as she was everything else. Judi doubted she would ever learn to be anything by halves. "They look terrible on you!" she shouted at Leonor. "And so does that dress! Mama would have been ashamed of you!"

The silence was deafening. They really were an incredible family, Judi thought, as she looked from one to the other of them. Not by a gesture did one of them betray that they had even heard Fabiola's outburst.

"It's getting late," Doña Maria said with a yawn, "and we have another late night tomorrow. I think it's time we all went to bed!" Her eyes twinkled suddenly as she saw that Judi was still caressing the pattern on her needlework box. "Mind you don't wear it out!" she teased. She yawned again. "Oh, I must be getting old! Would it be too much to ask you to see the little one to bed, Hudi? Good night all! *Buenas noches!*"

Judi and Fabiola went with her at once, leaving Don Joaquin and Leonor to their own devices.

"I hate her!" Fabiola ground out under her breath. "Hudi, you don't think Papa can really like her, do you?"

Judi stroked the little damascene box for good luck. "I hope not," she said, "but if he does, you'll have to learn to like her a little, too."

"Never, never, *never!*" Fabiola said flatly. "I'll go to England with you!"

Yes, thought Judi, and the sooner she went back to England the better, for the thought of Don Joaquin and Leonor together was breaking her heart. She rather wished that she could stamp her feet and rail at Leonor as Fabiola had. She helped Fabiola out of her dress and tucked her into bed, kissing her goodnight, and then she went to her own room and tried to pretend that nothing very much had happened to her after all, and that she wasn't in the least bit in love with Don Joaquin and wasn't likely to be.

Chapter Seven

Judi had never known another Christmas like it. Back in England she had always spent Christmas Day alone with her parents, helping her mother cook the traditional Christmas dinner and then eating far too much, followed by a walk with her father and an evening spent looking at the television. Here, she had other things to worry about. She was sorely tempted to go downstairs and have breakfast with Don Joaquin, yet she knew she could not. If she were ever alone with him again, it might not stop at a few kisses because, and she could admit this to herself, at least now, she had no defences against him.

The problem remained as to what she was going to do if he carried out his threat and brought his breakfast up to her room. The prospect made her feel hot and cold all over. She simply couldn't allow it! In a panic, she dressed herself and let herself out of the castle, walking through the almost empty streets as fast as her legs would carry her.

"Señorita, *un copa de vino?*"

Judi turned to see the proprietor of one of the wine bars eagerly trying to attract her attention. "It's too cold a day for you to wander about alone," he went on. "Come in and warm yourself."

It was pleasant to sit in the small cellar sampling the different wines they had to offer. She had had no idea that Spanish wines were so varied or so good. She sipped sherry, both sweet and dry, and then went on to the table wines while her host explained how some of them travelled well and could be taken back to England with her, whilst others would deteriorate if they were moved a few miles from where they had been grown and made.

By noon she was pleasantly warm, and very much at her ease. By this time, she thought, Don Joaquin would be safely in Leonor's company and she was free to return to the castle any time she would.

There was no one around as she made her way up to her room. She felt very much alone. If she had been less sleepy she would have felt very sorry for herself. She couldn't flatter herself that anyone would have missed her—perhaps Fabiola would have a little, but the others would be glad not to have to entertain her all day. She was sure Leonor would have barred her from the dance that night if she had had her way.

Judi lay down on her bed and, in a matter of moments, was fast asleep. When she awoke, it was because the maid was at the door, bringing her an assortment of cold meats and bread to keep her going until the formal dinner that evening.

"*Buenas tardes*, señorita! If you have a moment, the *patrón* wishes to see you in his study." She looked curiously at Judi, a sly excitement at the back of her eyes. "He has been looking for you all day. Where have you been?"

Judi leaned up on her elbow. "Is anyone with him?" she asked.

"*Sí, sí*, the Señorita Leonor—"

"Please be so good as to tell him I am busy now."

"Very well, señorita, just as you say." She stifled a smile. "But I don't think that the *patrón* will be too pleased." She curtsied and went quickly out the door, closing it softly behind her.

Judi waited until the maid was gone, then she pushed the tray away and burst into tears. Of course Leonor had been with him all day. She had probably been with him all night, too. She hated the two of them, but most of all she hated herself for caring what they did.

The ballroom had been transformed for the annual dance. Gone were the dust-sheets and the air of neglect that she had noticed earlier. Now the mirror-clad walls were polished, the chandeliers brilliant, and the floor carefully prepared for the night's entertainment.

Judi sat beside Doña Maria on one of the small gilt chairs. She had repaired the ravages of her tears as best she could, but she suspected that the Spanish woman had seen at a glance that something was wrong because she had gone out of her way to be kind to her despite all the many claims that were being made on her attention.

"Sit by me, Hudi, until I can find some partners for you." She smiled at her with real affection. "I expect these dances are strange to you. Never mind, everyone will want to teach you the steps. Don't let Joaquin stop you from enjoying yourself. He's been like a cat on hot bricks all day!"

Judi cast a swift look round the room. Leonor was clad in her favourite orange, a flamenco dress that displayed her legs in the front and had a small train at the back. She looked less than happy, but her proprietorial air towards Don Joaquin was just the same. Her hand was hooked over his arm as though she'd never let him go. Don Joaquin looked in a thoroughly bad temper. Perhaps he hadn't spent the day with Leonor after all.

She tore her eyes away from them, trying to concentrate on what Doña Maria was saying to her. Once started, she seemed to have a great deal to say about very little, but Judi was naturally kind and not for the world would she have wanted Doña Maria to know that she was slowly boring her to death.

"We always use the same local band. Joaquin likes these affairs to be very Castilian. Have you seen all the instruments they are using?"

"The guitars and the tambourines," Judi responded indifferently. "What are the other things?"

"*Zambombas*. Excuse me for just a moment, my dear."

The rhythm of the music changed to a stately waltz and Judi wished she had a partner after all. She liked to dance. It was one of the things she and David had had in common. Being much of a height, they had danced very well together, attempting all the latest steps long before they became fashionable amongst their friends. Was it because they had partnered each other so well when dancing that she had thought they would for life?

She looked up and found Don Joaquin standing before her. His eyes burned into her face and she felt herself colouring up beneath his angry gaze.

"Where were you all day?" he demanded.

"I—I went out!"

"So I heard," he observed gravely. "I've had people out looking for you ever since you didn't keep our tryst this morning."

She stirred uncomfortably. "It was hardly a tryst—" she objected. "You had Leonor to entertain you," she went on in a harder voice.

"Leonor and I understand one another perfectly." She was quite sure of that! "She is dancing with Stefano, *another* friend of hers. Will you dance with me?"

She inclined her head, quite unable to speak. Her whole body seemed to be floating on air as his arms went about her. Reality would return later and she would be miserable again but, for the moment, she was where she wanted to be and all was well with her world.

His arm tightened about her and the knot of excitement in her stomach flared through her veins. "I could strangle you with pleasure, *mi amor!* What did you think you were playing?"

They were so close that she could feel the movement of his muscles through her skirt. It was something to know that she had the power to excite him just as he did her. She gulped a breath of air.

"I didn't want to be alone with you," she confessed honestly. "Leonor—"

"This has nothing to do with Leonor! This is between you and me! I wanted to make the moment right for you, *bombón,* but you frustrated all my plans!"

She lifted her chin. "I don't want to be your mistress!"

A muscle twitched in his cheek. "Are you sure?"

He sounded every bit as dangerous as she had always known him to be. She trembled with the force of her own fears. No, she wasn't at all sure! It might be all the happiness she would ever know, for she didn't imagine that any other man would ever ignite her passions as Don Joaquin could with a touch of his hand. There would never be any other man for her that she could love as she now knew she loved him. She wanted to give herself to him, body and soul. She wanted him to be the first man with her but, even more, she wanted him to be the last.

"We don't live in the same world," she said unhappily. "I know, in Spain, it means nothing for a man to have a mistress as well as a wife, but in England—"

"Men cast off their wives and marry their mistresses? Would you prefer it if I thought of marriage as a temporary arrangement, to be terminated whenever I thought fit?"

"No, of course not!"

"Then where is the difficulty?" he asked her quietly.

There would be none if he wanted her to be his wife, but she could hardly tell him that. She had known right from the beginning that he would make a *suitable* marriage and that Leonor was the only suitable bride for him. She couldn't take what rightfully belonged to another woman.

She shrugged her shoulders. "You don't want to understand," she sighed.

"Then explain it to me," he invited her.

"I can't!" she cried out.

"My dear, sweet, silly Judi, if you had had breakfast with me as I asked you to it would all have been decided by now. Will you come out onto the verandah with me after this dance?"

She shook her head. His hand felt warm and masterful in the small of her back and she strained closer to him, unable to help herself. Where was the staid Judi now, who never lost her head? she wondered helplessly. He put his cheek against hers and her nostrils were filled with the male smell of him mixed with his after-shave, a spicy mixture of pine and coal tar soap. She shut her eyes, imprinting this moment onto her memory forever.

"I want to kiss you and have you say you're mine," he said roughly in her ear. "Is that so much to ask?"

She wanted it too! She hoped he'd never know how much she wanted it!

"I've always loved the waltz," she said in bright, social tones.

"Dancing is not enough. I want you in my bed!"

Her heart missed a beat at the thought. "You'll have to be content with what you have!" she reproved him.

"And will you be content with that?" he retorted.

Her breasts ached against the hard wall of his chest and she wasn't sure if it was her heart or his that was knocking so violently against her ribs. Perhaps it was both. The movement of the dance meant subordinating her body to the command of his and she rejoiced to have it so. If only the waltz would go on forever, but it was already drawing to an end. She dropped into a deep curtsey in response to his bow, her knees trembling so much she was obliged to clutch at his hand to retain her balance.

"Hudi, I must speak to you—"

She clenched her fists, tears welling up into her eyes. "No! How many times must I say it?"

"I must warn you—"

"Are you and Leonor going to announce your marriage tonight?"

He spread his hands in a despairing, very Spanish gesture. "*Bombón*, if you'd only listen! I long for you."

"Tell that to Leonor!"

"But it's you I love!"

Judi turned on her heel and walked away from him. How could he make a fool of her in this way? It wasn't kind! Perhaps she had misunderstood what he had said? She turned what she could remember of it over in her mind and decided she would be well rid of him once she had forgotten all about him. She told herself that would not be too difficult once she was in England again. But in her heart of hearts she knew it was a lie. She could never forget him!

She had almost reached her chair beside Doña Maria when Leonor caught up with her.

"Are you enjoying the dance?" the Spanish girl asked her, her eyes glittering with dislike.

"Are you?" Judi returned politely.

"Naturally. I feel responsible, though, for seeing that everything goes off well tonight. As an English woman you can't be expected to understand our little ways, so you won't mind if I drop you a word of advice. Don Joaquin dances with every one of his female employees at these Christmas dances. It would be a mistake to make too much of his dancing the waltz with you. Nor should you have consented without seeking Doña Maria's approval first. She is acting as your *dueña*, I suppose, as you have no family of your own here. So old-fashioned, of course, but she's not to know that girls do exactly as they like in England now. Some of us do in Spain, but it's best not to upset the older generation by being too obvious. You do understand what I'm saying, don't you?"

"Perfectly," Judi said acidly.

Leonor managed a bitter smile. "I thought you would. Don Joaquin may see fit to amuse himself with a little foreign nobody, but when it comes to marriage he knows where his duty lies. It's already arranged—"

"So I understand," Judi interrupted her. "You have nothing to worry about where I'm concerned, señorita. Don Joaquin means nothing at all to me!"

"How nice that would be if it were true," Leonor drawled. "You have my sympathy, my dear, but you can't have my man."

Judi's eyes, always a stormy grey, took on the aspect of a full-scale tempest at sea, but she was prevented from answering by Don Joaquin, deliberately moving towards her, bringing a very pretty young woman with him who looked so like Fabiola that she had to be a relation.

Don Joaquin took Judi's hand in his, ignoring her efforts to get away from him. "Don't be difficult, Hudi," he rebuked her as if it were the most natural thing in the world for him to hold her hand in public. Was he mad to make things so difficult for them both? *"Te presento a la Señora Pilar Haro, Teresa's younger sister."*

"Te" presento? Judi gulped. That was adding fuel to the flames with a vengeance. How could he address her in the familiar tense in public? Everyone would notice! Didn't he care?

"Encantada!" she whispered, trying to swallow the lump of dismay in her throat.

Pilar, however, seemed to think it perfectly normal. "I have heard all about you from Fabiola," she said with a smile. "You have quite an ambassador in my niece."

Judi glanced at Don Joaquin, seeking his guidance, but he was leading Leonor onto the floor. It was hard to bring her attention back to Pilar, but she seemed quite content to wait until Judi had herself in hand once again.

"May I call you Hudi? You must call me Pilar. I asked Joaquin to bring me over because he tells me that no one has thought to thank you properly for what you have done for Fabiola."

"It was nothing," Judi said automatically.

"Teresa wouldn't have thought so. I expect you've been told all about my sister?"

"The family thinks of her as a saint," Judi said.

"Perhaps she was one," Pilar sighed. "Saints are incredibly difficult to live with. The maddening thing was that one could never be angry with her because she always had an excellent, higher motive for everything she did. Being her sister was bad enough, but imagine being her daughter! Or husband!"

"Fabiola was very fond of her—"

"Oh, so were we all. I loved her as much as it's possible to love another woman, but I loved her even more at a distance, if you see what I mean. I am not a saint, and life means more to me than an opportunity to practise penances. Life is very good as it is, a nice mixture of family life, bad temper, beautiful clothes and the spice of gossip! Don't you like all those things?"

Judi found herself laughing. "Yes, I do."

"I thought so! Yet you would have understood Teresa better than I did. I'm told the chapel is exactly as she would have liked it and that that's your doing. You are Catholic, no? I suppose you had to be to design a Catholic chapel."

"Oh, no! Most of the work we do at the School is for the Church of England."

"Really? It was a lucky choice for us when Doña Maria came back from England with you!" She bent her head confidingly. "Poor lady, she is charming, but her taste is not at all Spanish. You have only to see how she dresses poor Fabiola and, indeed, herself. Her gown must be twenty years old at least and looks it! And Leonor's is indecent!"

Judi tossed up in her mind as to whether she could describe Leonor's dress of the previous evening to someone she had only just met, but Pilar was already following her own line of thought.

"You made Fabiola's gown entirely by hand?

It's fabulous! Teresa was always beautiful, but her little daughter is going to be something extraordinary! There's no lack of life there! Even her manners seem to be more gentle than when I last saw her, when she was forever interrupting and telling one what to do."

"I've never seen her—" Judi stopped, remembering Fabiola's reaction to Leonor last night.

Pilar made a face at her, obviously having heard all about it. "She wants you to like her, whereas for Leonor she has only a grand contempt!"

"Poor Fabiola!" Judi sighed.

But Pilar only smiled. "You have nothing to worry about, I promise you. Fabiola will come to me for a long stay as often as I can arrange it. Fortunately, my offspring are very placid and don't mind in the least being taken on route-marches and having orders barked at them. It does them good. I've often wondered why it is that little boys are so much more timid than little girls!"

Not having had any brothers, Judi had known few little boys, but she couldn't imagine that Don Joaquin had ever been timid, or that he would have taken kindly to a female cousin giving him orders. More and more, she wondered why he had ever submitted to his family's choice of bride when he had married Teresa. Family custom must be stronger than she knew if it had forced Don Joaquin to bend to his parents' wishes.

"He was very young," Pilar said gently. "I was only a child at the time, but I could see he was very much in love with Teresa. I think he loves her still. What neither of them understood was that there was no sexual passion in Teresa's love. If there ever had been in Joaquin's for her, it soon died of neglect. He won't make that mistake again." Judi rather thought not as she recalled the Spanish girl's flashy sexuality.

"Well, *bombón*, are you going to dance with me again?"

Judi stared, wide-eyed, into Don Joaquin's masterful face. She could feel Pilar's surprise at the stupid endearment and a great wave of burning colour rose into her face.

"Yes, go and dance with him," Pilar said kindly. "I've kept you talking far too long, but I had to tell you how delighted I am by the change in Fabiola." She kissed Judi lightly on the cheek and Judi could feel herself blushing again as Don Joaquin raised a mocking eyebrow at his sister-in-law's action.

"Another conquest, *querida*?"

She refused to look at him. "I like Pilar, yes," she said. "Shouldn't you be dancing with Leonor?"

"I've done all my duty dances."

She faltered in her step. "*I'm* a duty dance! I've been told how you dance with each of your female employees."

"Once is a duty dance; twice and it has another meaning."

"What meaning?" she asked, unable to restrain herself.

"What would you like it to mean? That it's the only way I can get you to talk to me? Or that it's the perfect excuse to hold you in my arms and feel your body against mine?"

She shouldn't have asked! "Leonor—" she began.

"Don't be discourteous, *mi amor*. At the moment I'm dancing with *you* and don't wish to be reminded of any other woman. Do you want to talk about your ex-fiancé?"

The backs of her hands prickled at the thought. She was increasingly glad that Don Joaquin was never likely to meet David. Poor David could never compete with the urgent masculinity of the Spaniard. He would look pale and fragile beside him. Even his gentle manners would make him seem ineffective beside Don Joaquin's arrogance.

She marshalled her thoughts together, intent on telling him that an ex-fiancé was quite different from a future one and that, moreover, David was not standing on the sidelines, glaring at every movement they made.

"I don't want to dance any more," she said aloud.

"Of course you do!"

His hand slipped over her back, fingering the top of her dress and on to her bare shoulders and neck. "Did you make this dress, too?" he asked.

She bowed her head. "Yes."

"What a talented girl you are!"

She knew he was only teasing her, but her heart warmed towards him. She badly wanted to link her hands together behind his head and pull his face down close against hers. Apparently, he wanted that too, for his hand in the small of her back drew her inexorably closer towards him until she could feel the hardness of his thighs against hers, and her fingers trembled in his.

"Pilar likes Fabiola's dress," she told him, managing a shaky smile. "Is she like her sister?"

"There's a portrait of Teresa hanging in one of the side-rooms. Why don't you judge for yourself?"

She thought it was another ruse to get her by herself and she shook her head sadly. "Not now. Some other time perhaps."

"What a prickly creature you are," he marvelled. "When will you allow me to have a word with you in private?"

"Not—not tonight!"

"Then let it be on your own head!"

But she knew quite well he had himself far too well in hand to go any further than he had already done to antagonise his bride-to-be. In fact, she had it in her heart to feel quite sorry for Leonor. She would be his wife, but would she ever be the mistress of his undivided heart?

A silence fell over the room and the dancing couples came to a stop, looking about them to see why the band had broken off in the middle of the romantic tune they were playing. Only Don Joaquin paid no attention, moving smoothly across the room to where his mother and his daughter were locked in a fierce, if whispered, battle of wills.

"What is it, Mama, Fabiola?" he asked them quietly, his expression lazy and quite unmoved by the interest they were attracting.

"Fabiola, no! There's an end to the matter!" Doña Maria hissed at her granddaughter. "Your father will make his own announcements!"

A mutinous look fell over Fabiola's face. "Just because I'm a *girl*," she said disgustedly. "You wouldn't say a word if I were a boy!"

"The fact remains you are not a boy!"

Don Joaquin put his arm round his daughter.

"And I'm very glad you're not one. What is it you want to do, *pequeña*?"

The child's eyes shone. "You know! What we were talking about earlier, Papa. You said you were going to tell everyone tonight! I want to make the announcement while Tía Pilar is here!"

Judi was afraid she was going to faint. She shut her eyes and wished the ground would open and swallow her up. He was going to tell them now he was betrothed to Leonor and the last of her hopes would be blighted. She had had no right to entertain those hopes, she knew, but she had found it increasingly hard to imagine him married to the Spanish girl. He had everything the wrong way round! It was Leonor who would make a better mistress than wife, except that she came from the right family and knew all the right people in Spain.

Don Joaquin's restraining hand slipped away from his daughter. "I don't think now is the right time," he began to explain to her, but Fabiola wasn't even listening.

"No, Fabiola!" Judi burst out, recognising the girl's determined expression and the equally helpless look on Doña Maria's face. "It's nothing to do with you!"

"But it is, Hudi, it is! Mama and I, and Santa Teresa of course, arranged it all! We saw how it was at once! Have you forgotten?" Her words could be heard in every corner of the ballroom and the guests were all smiling interest, all except Leonor who was rightly furious.

"Hush, Fabiola," Judi begged her.

But Fabiola had already turned to the room in

122

triumph, enjoying every bit of the drama she could wring out of having every eye on herself.

"You see, everybody, Papa met my friend Hudi in Avila—at Cuatre Postes. They had only to look at each other and the *flechazo*, the arrow of love, entered their hearts. Now that we're no longer in mourning for Mama, they'll be getting married. Abuela and I are very pleased!"

Doña Maria looked quite the opposite of pleased. She looked as if she could have strangled her granddaughter there and then.

"*Fabiola!*"

The child was half-frightened, half-annoyed at having her moment spoilt for her. She turned hopefully to her father.

"But it's true! Isn't it, Papa?"

Chapter Eight

Don Joaquin's grasp on her arm bruised her flesh.

"Go along with it for now, *querida*. Fabiola would never forgive us if we don't back her up."

"I won't—"

He bent his head, pressing his mouth on hers. For an instant she stood still, rigid with indignation, but the feel of his lips against hers undermined her determination. She leaned against him, no longer able to support herself on her shaking legs.

"Leonor—" she whispered.

"Leave her to me, *bombón*. Here is Pilar, ready to congratulate us on our good fortune."

The sarcastic turn of phrase hurt her. For a moment she had wondered if the whole thing hadn't been his idea, if he had wanted her for his wife after all. Now she knew that he had never entertained the idea—that he never would. She wasn't *suitable* in the way his wife would have to be, and nothing could make her so.

Pilar took note of the unshed tears in Judi's grey eyes and patted her lightly on the cheek with her closed fan in a gesture so familiar, so *Spanish*, that Judi could have cried in earnest.

"Tears? *Qué te pasa?* Don't you want to become one of us?"

Judi swallowed. "Oh, yes!"

"Of course she does!" Fabiola chimed in, pleased with herself.

Her aunt winked at the child. "I suppose you arranged it all?" she teased her. "You and your Mama?"

Fabiola nodded solemnly. "Mama would have approved of Hudi, don't you think?"

"*Claro!* She's the answer to all our prayers!" Pilar chuckled comfortably. "Except Leonor's," she added in an undertone. "*Mire!* Someone's in a fine rage now, and she's coming over here."

Judi could not face Leonor, not even with Don Joaquin beside her. It wasn't fair to either of them! She put up a hand and tried to unfasten Don Joaquin's fingers from round her arm, but as fast as she pried one loose another took its place.

"You can't run away now, Hudi. We all need you far too much! Leonor won't hurt you."

Oh, wouldn't she? Judi winced away from the fury in the Spanish girl's eyes, knowing it to be deserved. She should never have allowed matters to come to this. She should have gone back to England when Don Joaquin had first kissed her and she had known she was in danger of falling victim to his charms. But, if she had, how would she have carried out her commission where the chapel was concerned? If she wanted to be taken as a professional, she couldn't run away whenever the going got difficult!

Leonor descended on the family group with the appearance of a cat about to strike. "I can't believe my ears!" she hissed. "You must deny it at once, Joaquin! Half of our friends will have heard it already; and I refuse to be made a public spectacle at the whim of a child who should know better than to interfere where she's not wanted! Why isn't she in bed?" She turned on Judi, the frills of her orange dress shaking with her fury. "An English child would have been in bed long ago, Christmas Day or not! Why don't you take her upstairs now and put her to bed, seeing you're so fond of her?"

"Yes, of course I will," Judi agreed promptly, trying not to sound too relieved.

"You'll stay where you are!" Don Joaquin snapped. "The Christmas Dance is a family occasion and my daugher has every right to be here. Her mother always allowed her to stay until the last dance, even when she was in her cradle, and it's not for others who are scarcely family to tell me or Fabiola what to do!"

Judi would have withered into silence if such words had been addressed to her, but Leonor was made of sterner stuff. She shrugged her shoulders and, with her foot, flipped the train of her dress into a more attractive position.

"Very well. Fabiola must stay and listen while you tell everyone that she's a liar and a troublemaker. Of course you're not going to marry little Miss Nobody! I was prepared to overlook your tiresome little romance with her, but this! *Dios mío,* how can you do this to me?"

Don Joaquin became even more distant. "I wasn't aware that anyone had done anything to you."

But Judi thought she knew exactly how Leonor felt. It was a terrible thing to have happened —it was terrible for them both! She, herself, had been overwhelmed by Fabiola's unfortunate announcement, but how much worse it would have been if she had been expecting to become engaged to Don Joaquin herself, only to have someone else standing beside the man one loved and receiving the congratulations of all his intimate family.

"I'm terribly sorry, Leonor," she murmured.

"I'd prefer you didn't address me in such intimate terms!" the Spanish girl almost spat at her.

Pilar put a hand on her cousin's arm. "Come with me, Leonor," she commanded her briskly. "Everybody is looking at us and wondering why you are so distressed. This is not the moment for one of your famous scenes. Joaquin will talk to you about it later, *but not now.*"

"Why not now? He won't marry *La Inglesa!* Everyone knows that!"

"I don't know it," Fabiola said suddenly, enjoying the hated Leonor's discomfiture. "He certainly won't marry *you!*"

"Fabiola!" Doña Maria's fading tones spoke volumes for the embarrassing position in which the whole family had been placed. "You will apologise to your cousin. There's no reason to be rude to anyone."

Fabiola clung to her father's arm, a mutinous look on her face. "*She* was being rude to Hudi!" She raised her voice a few decibels. "She was being very *unkind* to Hudi!"

Judi bent towards the child. "I can look after myself, and so can your father. Poor Leonor—"

Leonor stamped her foot angrily. "I will not be called by my given name by a little nobody who's trying to steal my man—"

Judi didn't know what happened next. Don Joaquin moved with a suddenness that took them all by surprise and, one moment Leonor was there, and the next she had disappeared, walking away meekly on Don Joaquin's arm, her expression a trifle sulky but no longer twisted with rage and dislike for both Fabiola and Judi. Nor did Judi have any time to miss Don Joaquin. He was back beside her, almost before she had known he was gone, his arm possessively about her shoulders and with her hand firmly tucked into one of his.

"Will you dance, *bombón?*"

"Not if you call me by that ridiculous name!"

"But you are sweet, *mi amor,* and it's perfectly proper for your *novio* to call you anything he chooses."

"You're not my fiancé!"

"And you're every bit as argumentative as Fabiola at her worst," he murmured, his eyes laughing at her.

That reminded her. "What have you done with Leonor?" she demanded.

"What should I have done with her?"

One of these days, she vowed, she would get

the better of Don Joaquin and she would have the last word. She dwelt on the thought, savouring it as he swung her into the dance, not at all put out by the spasmodic applause of his guests who were delighted to see them dancing together. There wasn't one of them who seemed to think *La Inglesa* was an impossible choice for his wife. On the contrary, there were whispered congratulations to them both as they travelled slowly round the room, and all of them sounded sincere, almost as though they liked her and would be happy to see her as mistress of the *alcázar*.

"Leonor had reason to be angry," Judi said at last. "It was an unforgivable thing to do to her. It'll be your own fault if she never speaks to you again!"

"Not much danger of that," he replied calmly.

"Then she's better natured than I should be!" Judi said tartly.

"Ah, but you had reason to be sure of your position from the very beginning, no? You were Fabiola's choice, and Teresa's choice, the choice of the Saint herself if my family's to be believed!"

"Teresa is dead!"

"Fabiola is very much alive!"

"Yes, and that's another thing," Judi flared up. "How are you going to explain it to her when we get unengaged?"

He bent his head, touching the tip of her nose with his lips. "Are we going to get unengaged?"

"Of course we are! What else would we do?"

He smiled down at her. "If my daughter wants you for her stepmother, who am I to object? I could get married for worse reasons!"

She wanted to say something scathing, something that would put him in his place once and for all, but her Spanish deserted her and, in English, it wouldn't be the same thing. She contented herself by glaring up at him, but he showed no sign of noticing her displeasure and on the contrary, was looking remarkably pleased with himself and life in general. She soon abandoned the attempt to bring him to his senses. What did it matter, she reasoned to herself, if she were to pretend it was true for an hour or so? The only person it would hurt would be herself.

His eyes glinted with a sudden fire. "If you can dance this, you'll be half Spanish already!" he challenged her.

She laughed out loud, remembering how often she had danced these same steps with David. But it had never been the same in the past. She and David had moved well together, but with Don Joaquin she caught fire and nothing was too difficult for her. She whirled back and forth, drummed her heels on the floor, and arched her body to meet his in the classical, erotic movement of the flamenco dance.

When the dance came to an end they were alone on the floor.

"Bravo! Bis! Otra vez! Qué se repita!" came from all round the room, startling her into an awareness that they weren't alone.

"I think we've danced enough," she said firmly. "Thank you."

He bowed over her hand, turning her palm upwards and folding her fingers over the kiss he planted there. *"De nada,"* he replied politely.

* * *

There was only one answer to the mood she was in, Judi decided, and that was to work until she dropped. The sooner she completed the commission, the sooner she could get back to the safety of England. It was no good bemoaning the fact that she didn't want to go, just as it was no good feeling sorry for herself. England was her home and, of course, she would be glad to see it again. She looked out of her window, trying to pretend that she thought the scenery bleak and would much prefer the lush greenness of her native land. Only she didn't find the scenery bleak. She loved the pinkish soil and the very Spanish look of the buildings, with their shuttered windows and bulging walls that begged for a coat of fresh paint. Most of all she loved the roof tiles of the same pink as the soil, rounded like flowerpots, with weeds growing where they had cracked and broken.

Without her knowing it, Spain had become a part of her. When she left the castle, she would be leaving a very large part of herself behind also. What was the good pretending? She didn't want to go.

The nuns were surprised to find her already at work when they brought back the second of the altar cloths they had embroidered for her.

"The Señorita should be on holiday!" they exclaimed. "Surely she has a better use for her time just now than working herself to death?"

Used by now to being referred to in the third person by all except friends and relations, Judi merely smiled, hoping they had had a good Christmas.

"Not so exciting as yours!"

Judi stiffened, knowing that she was blushing.

Surely the news of Fabiola's unfortunate announcement hadn't spread so far so quickly?

"Shall we try the cloth on the altar?" she suggested.

The nuns whispered among themselves. Judi knew they thought her shy and approved of her modesty. If they only knew! She chewed on her lower lip, pretending that she didn't know they were talking about her. Nuns were women and women were gossips, she supposed. It would be kindly gossip, she was sure of that, but it wasn't *true!* Don Joaquin may have joked about taking Fabiola's choice of wife, but it wasn't as a wife that he really thought of her. He wanted her for his mistress, and what would the good nuns have to say to that?

"Padre Juan is pleased with the chapel?" the Reverend Mother asked at last. "His vestments fitted him properly, I hope?"

"The whole chapel looked lovely," Judi remembered. That had happened before. Everything now could be divided into before and after, she thought bitterly. She had had some chance of happiness before. What chance did she have now?

"So suitable that you are Catholic," the Reverend Mother went on happily.

It was the word suitable that did it. Judi didn't trust herself to say anything more on the subject, knowing that she was about to blow her top and nuns were really not the most suitable audience for such an interesting event. They wouldn't understand that she was desperate, that her whole world was falling apart all round her and that she was far from being *suitable* as a wife for Don Joaquin. His real fiancée thought she had behaved like a tart and Judi felt quite guilty enough for that to be true.

"I think I'll go to the back," she said aloud. "I'll be able to see what it looks like better from there."

"Just as you wish, señorita. Shall we put the new altar cloth on now?"

"Please," said Judi.

She was shaking so badly she was glad to sit down when she reached the back of the chapel. She had hoped that things would be better today, but they weren't, they were worse. What was she going to do? She couldn't go on pretending to be Don Joaquin's *novia* for a moment longer. If she did, she'd want to believe it was true so badly that she would never keep him out of her arms and her bed. She would grab at the chance of being close to him, even if it were only for a few days, and the prospect of going back to England with nothing but heartache and pain.

Then, almost as if she had conjured him up out of her own longing, he was just behind her, leaning against the doorpost, his dark eyes gleaming with an emotion that shamed her. It was Leonor he should be looking at like that, not her.

"What do you think, señorita?" the younger nun asked her.

She was shocked to discover she hadn't noticed that they had finished dressing the altar in a rich red silk, the colour of the martyrs' blood, heavily encrusted with the embroidered heraldic emblems of the family. Judi half-shut her eyes, forcing herself to concentrate. Yes, it was just right, she thought. Better than that, it was magnificent.

"It'll do very nicely," she said aloud.

Don Joaquin came further into the chapel. "It's splendid, ladies. We're absolutely delighted with the work you've done. We were overcome by the beauty of the chapel at the Christmas Mass. We hadn't expected it to look half so well. My congratulations!"

"The Señorita has an eye for these things," the Reverend Mother said with a smile. "We were just saying before you came in, how suitable it is that she is Catholic."

Suitable! There it was again.

"It wouldn't have changed anything if she had been Protestant, Sister," Don Joaquin said forcefully.

The nun looked resigned. "In these ecumenical times—"

"She would still be the same woman!"

The abruptness of his speech took both nuns by surprise. They exchanged amused glances, finding the whole exchange to be very romantic indeed.

"The lady of your heart?" the Reverend Mother suggested sweetly.

"Exactly," said Don Joaquin. "And my daughter's friend, of course."

Judi could bear no more. The lady of his heart, indeed! He might want to make love to her, but he no more wanted her on a long term basis than she—she— Oh, how could he do this to her? Didn't he realise how miserable he was making her?

She waited until the nuns had left, bowing and smiling, before she made her announcement. "I'm going back to England!"

He gave no sign of having heard her, but

walked briskly up the aisle to sit beside her. "Are you ready to talk now? he asked.

"No, I'm not!" She sniffed angrily. "I'm surprised you have the nerve to suggest it," she added in a fierce whisper.

"We have things to talk about," he pointed out. "Are you afraid to be alone with me, *bombón?*"

"Certainly not!"

"Then why are you hiding yourself away, working when no one else is working, and talking about rushing back to England at breakneck speed?"

"Because I don't want to talk to you! There's nothing to talk about!"

He raised an eyebrow in mocking enquiry. "Nothing?"

"Nothing!" she insisted. "If you want to talk to someone, go and talk to Leonor!"

He gave an exaggerated sigh. "Funny how you always drag Leonor into everything," he remarked.

"*I* drag her in? I don't have to! She was already here long before I came! And we all know what she was doing here!"

His smile was slow and showed how sure he was of himself. "Fabiola doesn't like her," he pointed out.

"She hasn't tried to make the child like her, but she's completely *suitable* in every other way that I can think of."

His smile grew broader. "How young and innocent you are, *chiquita.* Sometimes I think even Fabiola knows more about life than you do."

"Being Spanish, I expect she does," Judi agreed dryly.

He laughed out loud, drawing the nuns' eyes to them. "This isn't the right place to talk—"

"No, it's not!"

"Then will you come to my study, or shall I go to your room with you?"

Judi grasped the seat of her chair on either side of her knees, holding onto it as if her life depended on it.

"I'm not going anywhere. I haven't anything to say to you. I'm not going to marry you and that's that! I'll explain matters to Fabiola somehow—at least she meant kindly by me, but marry you I will not!"

He sat back in his seat, very much at his ease. "Why not? You're happy living in the castle, aren't you?"

She was cautious, seeking the trap in the question. "I like the castle, yes," she agreed.

"Well then, why do you want to run away?"

Judi was speechless with indignation. Didn't he *know*? She looked down at her lap and saw her knuckles shining white, so tightly was she hanging onto the wood.

"Is it Fabiola?" he pressed her. "Do you mind having a ready-made daughter before you have a chance to have any children of your own?"

"Of course not!" she said gruffly.

"Then is it marriage itself you're afraid of?"

She had never heard anything so ridiculous in her life. "I can't imagine why I ever thought the Spanish to be a romantic nation!" she exploded. "You can think of nothing but practicalities. You have as much emotion as David had in his little finger, and that isn't saying much! But at least he was *kind!*"

Don Joaquin's eyes narrowed dangerously. "I don't feel kindly towards you," he said flatly.

"I know that!"

"I imagine you should. You have every reason to know that if I told you what I wanted to do with you, I'd bring a blush to your cheeks and we'd end up not talking to each other at all. Besides, you hardly seem to be in need of my sympathy when you can get all hot and bothered about nothing all by yourself!"

"About nothing?" she gasped.

"Nothing much. I can understand your annoyance with Fabiola at making such a public announcement at such a time, but it wasn't so very unwelcome to you as you pretend. If you were honest, you'd admit you want me quite as much as I want you."

She began to tremble inwardly. If he was going to pursue that tack, she wasn't at all sure she could withstand him.

"What are you going to do about Leonor?" she asked abruptly.

"Leonor need not bother you, Hudi. This is between you and me. Nobody else comes into it in the end."

"I'm not going to bed with you!"

Her words startled her quite as much as they did him. His eyes crinkled with amusement, but there was quite another emotion reflected in his eyes.

"Hadn't you better wait until you're asked?"

She stared at him, her eyes as grey as the sea in winter. She was as bewildered now as she had been angry before. "I thought—" she began.

"You think too much! If you followed your

instincts, you wouldn't need to think at all. You'd take what you're offered and be thankful."

Really, that was too much. "It would depend what I'm offered!" she retorted bitterly. "And as for making a fuss about nothing, is it nothing that you don't deny it when Fabiola says we're engaged to be married? Is it nothing that Leonor should say what she did about me?

He put his forefinger across her indignant lips. "Are you really that upset?" he asked, a distinct edge to his voice. "Tell me about it."

"I don't want to marry you!" she said, and thought not without love on his side as well as hers. He might want her body, but he wasn't in love with her. He was in love with Leonor.

His arm descended with a crushing embrace about her shoulders. "I could change your mind about that," he threatened, sounding as angry as she had been earlier.

"How?"

She was totally unprepared for the speed with which he pulled her against him, his mouth taking hers in a kiss of bruising intensity. For an instant she held herself aloof, but the familiar magic sang in her blood, the agonising knot of misery exploding in her breast. Her lips parted beneath the demands of his as she moulded her body to his, rejoicing in her own surrender. She never would win if he could touch her. She had only to see and smell the warm male scent of him to want to be in his arms. She ought to be ashamed to feel like this about another woman's man, but when he kissed her, she was conscious only of him.

"Joaquin, let me go!" she begged him.

"Never, *bombón!* Saint Teresa would never

allow it, despite your lack of faith in her, and in her own chapel, too. You'll have to get used to her interest if you stay in Spain. Every Spaniard looks to the saints to arrange everything for them."

Judi chewed on her lip. It was outrageous that he should kiss her like that in his family's chapel, as if he really did wish to marry her and have the blessing of the Church on their union. He couldn't be allowed to get away with it.

"I hate you!"

"Do you, *mi amor*? You won't for long. You have too much fire and passion not to agree to be mine. But don't keep me waiting, *bombón*, because I'm not a patient man. With Teresa I had to be, but with you—" He paused, his eyes alight with his desire for her— "With you, I couldn't be patient if I tried!" He bent his head and kissed her again, her lips, the tip of her nose and then her lips again. "Besides, whatever would Fabiola say if I didn't keep you by my side now?" he added with a laugh.

Chapter Nine

"I'm not going to marry you and you're not going to have me any other way!"

She said the words in English, in a breathless whisper that betrayed some of the agitation she was feeling.

Don Joaquin switched easily into English also. "My dear girl, is that meant to be a challenge?"

Her mouth was dry with fright. *"No!"*

He took her hands in his. "Are you sure?"

She bowed her head. "I don't want to have anything to do with you."

"So you say with your lips, but your heart says something different." He pulled her closer against him, "Come to my room now, *bombón*, and let me make love to you."

"Certainly not!" She licked her lips, very conscious of his hand on her thigh. "And when I think how badly you've treated Leonor, I'm surprised you should have the audacity to ask me," she added, thus spoiling the finality of her refusal.

"Leonor has nothing to do with you and me."

"But she has!"

"Tell me about it," he invited her. His hand squeezed her waist with an insolent familiarity. The nuns had gone, but the chapel was hardly the place for this. She tore one of her hands free, but somehow she found herself clutching his wrist instead, as if she wanted to keep it against her for as long as possible.

"Joaquin—"

"Admit you want to make love with me." He smiled deliberately into her passion-clouded eyes. "You do, don't you, *querida*?"

"I can't!"

His expression softened to one of amused affection. "Why can't you?"

"I didn't come here to fall in love. I came to Spain to do a job, and when it's finished I mean to return to England and—and—"

Her voice died away, defeated, as his fingers bit into her flesh. "You're still hankering after that ex-fiancé of yours. Is that it?"

"David?" She was astonished. It seemed a long time since she had given him a thought. She had almost forgotten about him. She had thought she loved David, but compared to what she felt for Don Joaquin she knew she had been deceiving herself. David had never rendered her witless with a mere touch. She would never have sat in a chapel with him, wondering if she would have the strength of mind not to go to bed with him. "David is probably married by now."

"What's that got to do with it?" Don Joaquin demanded. "If *you* were married to him, I'd still want to make love to you!"

Her eyes flashed, her indignation giving steel to her resolve. "I wouldn't allow it for one minute! That's where we differ." She rose to her feet on shaking knees and looked down at him. "And I won't allow it now," she added grandly, and made a firm movement towards the door. "I shall be going back to England in the morning."

He leaned forward, supporting himself with his elbows on his knees, and shook his head at her.

"Hudi, I won't let you go!"

"Then you'll have to lock me in!"

A small smile tilted the corners of his mouth. "Don't tempt me, darling! Nothing would suit me better than to lock you in and throw away the key! I could make you very happy if I did! You wouldn't deny me your bed for long, *mi amor!*"

"And how many others would I share you with?" she shot at him.

The arrogant slant of his head confused her and she very nearly sat down again. Fortunately, she realized in time the dangers of that course, and instead she took a hasty step away from him.

"That would depend on the welcome you gave me."

He was completely impossible! He had no morals at all! So why she should be tempted to give him a welcome he'd never forget was totally beyond her. It was Leonor he loved, Leonor he meant to marry. She would do far better to remember that and forget all about the leaping

142

delight in her veins whenever he came close to her. He was not—and never would be—hers. Not even for a stolen night or two.

"Please don't," she said aloud.

"Tempted?" he mocked her. "Why won't you admit you want me?"

"It wouldn't be right!"

He stood up also. "When I hold you in my arms it feels very right to me."

She refused to look at him. He was too precious to her. "Spanish aristocrats may be able to make their own rules and get away with it, but lesser mortals—"

"What rule says I can't have you?"

She was flummoxed that he should ask. How dared he? She tilted her chin to a stubborn angle.

"If you can't understand that, at least you can understand how much more *suitable* Leonor is for your consideration! Why don't you go to her?"

"Perhaps I will, if you don't stop throwing her in my face every few minutes," he retorted soberly. "Why is it, Hudi, that we can't talk together for a few minutes without your flying off the handle?"

"Because you never understand anything!" she cried out.

The sound of her heels on the floor of the corridor gave her courage as she hurried to gain the stairs up to her room. They sounded as if she knew where she was going. They almost sounded cheerful and not at all heart-broken.

She came to a full stop at the foot of the stairs, her breath suspended as she listened for his footsteps following hers, but there was nothing to hear but the enveloping silence in her wing of the castle. It showed how little he felt for her, she decided, that he could let her go so easily. He probably had gone to Leonor, and it was her own fault if he had. Other women settled for something less than marriage, so why couldn't she?

The view from the window in her bedroom, previously an unfailing source of tranquility, now only added to her restlessness. She ought to put on a coat, go out and enquire about ways and means of going back to England, she told herself. But she didn't want to leave Spain. She *never* wanted to leave Spain. It would be like being driven from paradise to never see Don Joaquin, or even Fabiola and Doña Maria, again.

Judi made an effort to distract herself from her troubles by changing her dress, choosing one of her favourites, a pale yellow linen, cut in simple lines which accentuated the rise of her breasts and the narrowness of her waist. She looked at herself long and hard in the mirror, wishing she had worn it earlier. But how could she have known that Don Joaquin would see her in the chapel?

She would not think of him anymore. She made herself remember every detail of the new altar cloth, reviewing it critically to decide if she wanted any alterations made in it. The nuns had done a good job, carrying out her instructions to a tee. She thought that if they did the others as well, she would have no complaints, and she didn't think the family would have any either.

The knock at the door caught her by surprise.

"Pase," she called out, expecting it to be the maid.

"Hudi, it's me. I can't get in."

Judi went over to the door and unlocked it. She had no recollection of turning the key earlier and she couldn't think why she had done so. She had known Don Joaquin wasn't following her. Was it possible that she had hoped he would?

"Why did you lock the door?"

Fabiola's indignation came as a tonic to her spirits. "Goodness knows," she said. "I didn't know I had."

"Oh. Are you all right? You look queer."

"Queer?" Judi repeated. "I was just thinking how nice I look in this dress."

"Yes, you do," Fabiola agreed, without much interest. "You always look nice though. Abuela says you have better taste than Tía Leonor." She made a face as she mentioned the hated name. "She says, thank God you're not flashy. The way you dress isn't out of line in any way."

"Don't tell me she thinks I dress *suitably*?" Judi demanded in dangerous tones. She could have torn the dress off her back there and then.

Fabiola nodded vigorously. "She won't admit it, but she's awfully glad Papa changed his mind about marrying Leonor—"

"Are you sure he has?" Judi interrupted her.

"He can't marry both of you!"

It was a child's logic, Judi reminded herself. Fabiola wanted it to be so. Goodness knows, she had done her best to make it so. But nothing was really changed. All that had happened was that her father hadn't wanted to contradict his little daughter in public. At the appropriate moment he would still marry Leonor, forgetting he had ever wanted Judi, even on the temporary basis as his mistress.

She put an arm round Fabiola, hugging her to take the sting out of her words. "You shouldn't have made that announcement, little one. Your father let it go, but it's put us in a very awkward position. I know you don't want Leonor to be your stepmother—"

"There's no danger of that now!"

"I shouldn't be too sure of that."

The child's face fell. "But he *promised* he wouldn't."

"It's true he knows you don't like her very much, but she would probably make a very good wife for him."

Fabiola hid her face against Judi's arm. "Mama didn't make Papa a very good wife."

"You can't know that!" Judi exclaimed.

Fabiola looked at her kindly. "Mama didn't like being touched, not by *anyone*. She didn't go all red when Papa came into the room. You like it when he kisses you, don't you?"

Judi sat down on the end of the bed, unable to cope. "I shouldn't like it," she said at last.

Fabiola looked at her, both amused and curious. "Papa likes it, too! He told me so."

"He had no right—"

"Why shouldn't he tell me things?" Fabiola demanded. "I'm the closest relative he has."

Judi pulled herself together with difficulty. "Is that what you came to tell me?" she asked with some asperity.

Fabiola looked guilty. "No. Abuela sent me to find you. She wants to see you in her sitting-room, only she said to be very careful how I asked you. I wasn't to barge in, and I wasn't to upset you, and I was to say please, and if you didn't want to see her to tell you she would quite understand." Fabiola paused importantly. "You see, she thinks you're going to marry Papa, too."

"Only because of your announcement."

Fabiola shook her head. "Papa's been talking to her about you. He said you'd left him flat in the chapel. Did you, Hudi? With Papa, you know, it's much better not to make him angry, and he sounded very angry when he was talking to Abuela!"

"That's because he doesn't want to marry me." Judi looked down at her hands, loosely linked in her lap, and saw that they were shaking. "And I certainly don't want to marry him!"

"Are you coming to see Abuela?"

Judi nodded. "I'd better get it over with. What are you going to do?"

"I'll come with you as far as Abuela's room."

Judi suspected the girl had been told to escort her all the way back in case she should change her mind on the way. What a ninny they thought her! What a ninny she was—unable to make up her mind to any course of action and stick to it for two consecutive moments put together. At least she had no choice but to tell Doña Maria herself that there would be no wedding, no *unsuitable* wedding at any rate, and that therefore there was no need for her to warn Judi off her son once again. Judi had got the message the first time.

She felt hot and cold by turns as she knocked on the door of the sitting-room. Doña Maria opened it herself, drawing her into the room and into her scented embrace at the same time.

"My dear, you mustn't think you have to knock at any doors in this castle. Come in, come in! I thought we might have a cup of tea together. The English always drink tea when anything happens to them, isn't that right? And what could be more exciting than for you to get yourself engaged to my son? Therefore, we shall have a cup of tea together now."

Judi wondered what she would say if she told her she preferred coffee. The thought sustained her all the time she was being kissed on either cheek and led across the room to a chair by the open fire.

"We have so much to talk about," Doña Maria went on, uttering small, excited little sounds all the while. "So very much!"

Judi sat down, not knowing what else to do, while the Spanish woman fussed about her, plumping up cushions and repeatedly ringing the bell for the maid to bring their tea.

"Now," Doña Maria said at last, triumphantly seating herself opposite Judi. "Now there is nothing to disturb us, my dear. What shall we talk about first? I do hope you're not going to insist on getting married in England. Padre Juan is convinced that he'll be asked to officiate and he'll be terribly disappointed if you want anyone else. He's become so fond of you—as we all have—while you've been working on the chapel."

Judi opened her mouth, waiting for the flood of words to cease before she could get a word in edgewise.

"There isn't going to be any wedding. At least," she amended, "I'm not going to be the bride. I expect to be asked before I agree to marry anyone—and not by the child of the first marriage, either! Besides, my parents would want to see me married."

"So they shall," Doña Maria agreed. "Did you think we wouldn't ask them?"

"Ask them to what? There isn't going to be any wedding!"

Doña Maria stared at her, her mouth hanging open. "Hudi, don't you understand? There has to be a wedding! Why should you want to refuse? Don't you want to marry my son?"

Judi refused to commit herself. "Fabiola—"

"No, no, my dear, this has nothing to do with Fabiola. She made the announcement last night, I know, but it wasn't *she* who put the announcement in the paper and in the *London Times*."

"Who did?" Judi asked weakly.

Doña Maria hitched up her ill-fitting black skirt with one hand while she passed Judi her tea with the other. "We think it was Leonor," she said brightly. "*Not* from the best intentions, I'm afraid. I think she meant to embarrass Joaquin—and you, too. But he isn't at all embarrassed, I'm thankful to say. When I told him, he said that now he wouldn't have to bother locking you up and throwing away the key; that she had done it for him—"

"The man is monstrous!" she gasped.

Doña Maria chuckled. "You mustn't mind, my dear. I have been married myself."

"That's not the point. What must he think of

me? He treats me like a chattel. How does he know I want to marry him? So far he's only suggested I should become his mistress!"

"My dear!"

"I refused," Judi went on, her angry momentum lost.

"That wasn't very clever of you," Doña Maria said disapprovingly. "Joaquin is my son so I can't be sure, but his father was a splendid lover!"

"Perhaps he was faithful to you," Judi sniffed.

"Some of the time. He never neglected me, and he was kind enough to make me feel he wanted me until the day he died. In fact, I can't be sure if he was faithful to me or not. It's not of great moment either way. I was special to him in a way no other woman could be."

"You were his wife."

Doña Maria smiled gently, almost complacently. "But, my dear, you will be Joaquin's wife."

Not without love. It always came back to that. If Joaquin loved her even a tenth as much as she loved him, she would have married him without another word despite Leonor's prior claim. But without love she could not!

"My parents don't buy the *Times,* and I won't be blackmailed into marrying your son."

For once Doña Maria was impatient with her. "Will you allow Leonor to call your bluff? I thought English girls had more spirit!"

Judi shook her head sadly. "Not this one. Thank you for the tea, but it won't do, you know. I can't marry Joaquin and I won't be his mistress. There's nothing else for me to do but go back to England, is there?"

"You really won't stay? Not even for Fabiola's sake?"

She couldn't stay without love and there had been no word of that. "I'll go and pack my things," she said aloud.

Doña Maria shrugged her shoulders. "You must do as you think best. I'm disappointed."

"I thought you wanted Leonor as your daughter-in-law?"

Doña Maria pursed up her lips. "I want my son to be happy in his marriage and Fabiola to have a mother she can love." She rose to her feet, her head held high very much in her son's manner. "I'll wish you goodbye now, señorita. Someone must be here to console the little one—and to tell Joaquin that you've gone."

The finality of the words touched Judi to the quick. Could she bear to go? Could she bear to stay?

"I may not be able to book my ticket today," she began uncertainly.

"I'm sure you'll manage somehow."

"Yes," Judi agreed. "I suppose I will. Goodbye—"

Doña Maria inclined her head in acknowledgement. "Go with God, señorita, and remember, we each have to do what is right."

Judi left the room reluctantly, puzzling over the Spanish woman's last remark. Had she ever doubted that Doña Maria would do what she felt to be her duty? Or Joaquin either? He would marry Leonor once she was out of the way and they were welcome to one another. She had to believe that or she would never find the courage to leave, but would go running to Joaquin, prepared to accept anything he cared to offer her.

She had to think of her future, and what future would she have with Joaquin in love with another woman?

Judi went to her room by way of the chapel. She slipped inside, looking back over her shoulder in case anyone should have seen her, but there was no one in sight. The spectacle inside that met her eyes sent a wave of shock through her being. Someone had removed the new scarlet altar cloth from the altar and had torn it into pieces, littering it round the floor. It was then that she saw Padre Juan standing in the doorway of the vestry.

"What happened?" she gasped.

"We must not blame anyone, Hudi. Sometimes people are given more than they can bear at one time—and this is the result."

"But an altar cloth!"

He came and helped her pick up the pieces. "The person concerned has no true belief. The altar cloth is ruined because it's connected with you, I think."

"*Leonor?*"

"She is not yet reconciled to your marriage—"

"She doesn't have to be! There won't *be* any marriage!"

The old priest sighed. "Perhaps that's just as well. What will you do, Hudi?"

"I'm going back to England."

"Don't take any bitterness with you."

Judi held out the torn pieces of cloth. "Wouldn't you be bitter if someone hated you as much as this?"

Padre Juan took them from her. "Leonor is impulsive, a creature of the moment. The cloth can be copied by the nuns and made as good as new. Your work will survive your presence amongst us. You must have no fear of that."

But Judi couldn't get the bad taste out of her mouth. Leonor had been determined to get rid of her—and she had certainly succeeded. But she had gone about it in a strange way—Judi simply couldn't imagine herself making a public fool of the man she wanted to marry. She would never have taken the risk of putting an announcement in the paper to bring him to heel, no matter how hurt she had been. Judi could only suppose that Joaquin had told her there was no truth in Fabiola's announcement, but that it had done little to assuage Leonor's rage at being supplanted even for a moment. She had been angry enough for anything, and would have wanted to punish both Joaquin and Judi for allowing Fabiola's announcement to stand so as not to disappoint the little girl. She probably knew how much it would cost the proud Joaquin to have had to make a more public rebuttal of his daughter's claim than he would have had to do at the dance. It would be better than a public apology —it would be a public avowal of Leonor as the first woman in his life for all to see!

What Judi could not understand was the spite that had brought Leonor to the chapel and the ruin of the altar cloth. Judi thought of it as Saint Teresa's chapel. Leonor thought of it as *Judi's*, and had seen it as a way of clearing out the English woman's influence in the castle once and for all. It was the only possible explanation for what was otherwise a piece of totally wanton destruction.

Well, despite her methods, Leonor had won. Judi was going and she would never come back. Leonor might suspect *La Inglesa* had left her heart behind in Spain, but it would be of little interest to her. Judi wondered if Leonor had a heart at all. The Spanish woman was violent, touchy and greedy, but she would be sweet enough once she was Joaquin's wife. Perhaps Jouaqin, too, would be content with that.

It was a lonely departure. Judi half hoped she would see Fabiola, and that the little girl might come and see her off. In that she was disappointed. Even the maids had gone to their own quarters and would not be back on duty again for at least an hour.

Judi took a tight grip on her suitcase and walked, for the last time, down the circular staircase that led to her rooms. The polished wooden floors of the formal rooms downstairs looked cloudy after the use they had been put to the night before. Even the Arab-style, decorated ceilings looked less brilliant than she knew them to be. It felt as though the whole castle was in mourning for her going, though she knew that she was but a passing stranger who had no right to put down her roots and live out her days within its solid, ancient walls.

The town was deserted. A donkey munching its way through a bag of greenery was the only creature in the street, apart from herself. She turned the corner into the square and saw a bus parked alongside the *bodega* where she had bought the bottle of wine for the policeman. The driver sat hunched in his seat, smoking a cigarette. He stood up when he saw her, opening the automatic doors and taking her suitcase from her. It was only when Judi stepped inside that she realised this was a much grander coach than the local bus which plied its way between the town and Madrid each day.

"Are you going to Madrid?" she asked the driver.

"Eventually. We start from there. We finish there."

Judi sat down in the rear of the bus. Perhaps the local bus wouldn't be running that day. There was no one whom she could ask and, even if there had been someone, they would have answered whatever they thought would please her, not wanting to witness her disappointment if they told her the truth. She would stay where she was, she decided, if she had enough loose money to pay for her ticket. If Don Joaquin came after her, he wouldn't be able to find her and she would be free of him forever.

Once in Madrid, she would find a cheap hotel and cash some traveller's cheques to pay her bill and buy her plane ticket back to England. She had spent remarkably little since coming to Spain so, even though she hadn't yet received payment for her work, she would still have ample money to cover her expenses until she was safely home.

The small group of tourists came out of the *bodega* in the wake of their multilingual guide, a young woman of striking looks who stood shivering on the pavement as she watched them all climb in and return to their seats.

The doors swished shut and the coach pulled out of the square. Judi shut her eyes against the tears that threatened to spill down her cheeks. When she opened them again, the guide was counting her charges, coming steadily towards her down the aisle.

Chapter Ten

"You have a ticket for Toledo, señorita?"

"No," Judi admitted. "I want to get to Madrid."

The guide hid her exasperation as best she could. "You're not Spanish, señorita, are you? Perhaps you don't understand that this is a tourist bus. We have been on an excursion to El Escorial Palace this morning. This afternoon we go to Toledo for lunch and a visit to the city. It'll be late before we get back to Madrid."

"It doesn't matter," Judi said indifferently. "How much does the ticket cost?"

The girl visibly cheered up when she saw that Judi meant to pay for the full excursion. "You need only pay for Toledo. Are you English or American?"

"English," Judi told her.

"We have one other American lady with us so

you'll have an English explanation as well as the Spanish. She will be glad of your company. All the rest of us are Spanish."

Without interest, Judi promised to look for the American. She didn't want to talk to anybody just then. In fact, she doubted if she would ever want to talk to anyone again.

"My name is Carmen," the guide went on cheerfully. "If you've never been to Toledo, you have a treat in store. Enjoy yourself—!"

Judi was glad when Carmen went back to the front of the coach and reached for the microphone, blowing on it in a businesslike manner to make sure it had been switched on. She hoped they had all enjoyed their break in the small *bodega*. Now they were going past the town's *alcázar*, still in private hands and owned by the same family who had built the fortress as long ago as the eleventh or twelfth century. It was a great pity they couldn't see the inside because she had been told it had been superbly modernised and was extremely comfortable despite its great age.

The guide paused and then repeated the whole thing in English. She followed that by a brief comment on the death of Doña Teresa the year before, but that now there was happier news. She had been told in the *bodega* that the *patrón* was to marry again, this time to an English woman whom they all knew well in the town. It was to be a splendid wedding, with the whole town *en fête*, and with all of the most famous families of Spain there.

A romantic sigh went round the bus. What would they think if they knew the same *La Inglesa* they were talking about was cowering on the bus just behind them? She sniffed pathetically as they rounded the corner and the castle came in sight. She would remember how it looked forever, she thought. When she had first seen it she had thought of Walt Disney and Snow White, but now she thought only of Don Joaquin. How could she bear to live without him? How could she bear the loneliness, now that she had met him? She had thought she knew all about unhappiness when David had told her he was in love with somebody else, but now she knew that all that had been dented had been her pride. She had enjoyed David's company, nothing more than that, but parting from Joaquin was like being torn in two and knowing she would never be whole again.

The drive to Toledo was punctuated by remarks from the guide, pointing out the historic spots. Under other circumstances Judi would have enjoyed the trip. She had no preconceived picture of Toledo, and she found it interesting that nobody really knew why Philip II had changed the capital city to Madrid unless it was because it was nearer to his palace-cum-monastery at El Escorial. Toledo remained the spiritual capital, an enclosed city which had changed little over the centuries. Nowadays, when a house was taken down, it was replaced by its exact replica, and nobody would have thought of changing the hundreds of secret passages that ran between the houses and streets, adding to both the beauty and the claustrophobic atmosphere of the place.

They first went around the city, crossing a bridge and climbing a hill opposite to the restaurant where they were to have lunch.

"I wish we could have seen that castle," the American woman said as they sat down. "It could have come out of a fairy tale! If it's as gorgeous on the inside as it is on the outside, what a lucky person this English woman is! A compatriot of yours, I guess?"

Judi felt she could safely say yes to that.

Their first course was brought to them, and a young boy came to take their orders for drinks. Judi ordered a mineral water for herself, sneaking a glance at her watch. It was already nearly three o'clock. At the castle they would be finishing their meal rather than just beginning it.

The American ordered herself a compari-soda, then changed her mind and had a Spanish brandy instead.

"I'm getting a taste for it," she said easily. "It's not as strong as French brandy and doesn't send you to sleep for the rest of the afternoon. Have one on me, if you like."

Judi refused the offer with a smile. "Thank you, but I seldom drink. I never drank wine before I came to Spain."

"And then you found you liked it?" the American teased her.

"I had a glass in Segovia with—with someone I know. I liked it very much."

"It sounds as though you liked him even more."

"It could have been a she," Judi remarked with spirit.

"Not with that look on your face. Where is he now? Did you leave him behind in that town where you joined the tour?"

"In a way," Judi admitted. "I only went with him to look after his daughter."

"Bad luck!" The American made a face. "The best ones are always married!"

Judi was about to tell her that this particular man was a widower, but she thought better of it. She took a mouthful of soup and tried to think of other things. Why weren't there more English-speaking tourists about? Probably most of them were home with their families for the holidays. The thought saddened her. "Is your family with you?" she said aloud.

"Not this trip. I'm working here. I'm in the travel business and this was the only time I could get away to see what it's like on the ground. All my family have had is a phone call every night I've been away. How about you?"

"I'm here on a job, too."

"Oh yes? What d'you do?"

"Needlework. I came to refurbish a private chapel. It hadn't been in use since the Civil War and I had to design new vestments—everything —so that it can be used again."

The American woman frowned. "Funny," she remarked, "the guide said something like that about the new wife at the castle." Her eyes narrowed. "You got on there," she added slyly.

"I didn't hear the guide say anything about her except that she was English," Judi said firmly.

"She'd turned the microphone off," the American explained. "Are you sure you don't know more than you're saying?"

"Quite sure," Judi said with decision.

She couldn't help noticing, however, that the American woman must have said something to their guide because, shortly after they had been taken up to the high square of the city in preparation for the long walk down through the narrow streets, Carmen came over to her, eyes snapping with curiosity, to ask if she had ever been inside the castle they had passed that morning.

"It looks very like the one in Segovia," Judi complied. "I'd love to visit there sometime. Is it true that the Catholic kings used to live there most of the time?"

Carmen looked at her thoughtfully. "Yes, it's true. It must have been very cold in the winter."

Judi looked about her, admiring the patterns on the brick walls as any other tourist would. "Does it get very cold here?"

Carmen shivered to make her point. "Winter is only just beginning! We may have some snow before the afternoon is out, but it'll be lovely and warm in the coach when we go back to Madrid."

She turned to her group, beckoning them to stay close behind her. "It's very easy to get lost in these narrow passages," she warned them. "Please make sure that you always keep me in sight. If you do get tired, or lost, or want to drop out for any reason, you'll find the coach down at the bottom, by the river."

She went on with her directions, but Judi was no longer listening to her. What fun this would have been if Don Joaquin had been with her! All her life she had longed to visit the city of El Greco, to see the paintings she had always admired in reproduction, paintings as distinctive as any others she had ever seen, with their elongated bodies and female hands, and that curious, lost look that so many of his sitters had had.

Following their guide, they began the long

trail, walking at a brisk pace partly to keep warm and partly to get through the heavy schedule that had been mapped out for them. Judi began to wish she had not changed her dress earlier, and especially not her shoes, which she quickly found to be unsuitable on the uneven surfaces of the pavements and narrow roads.

The Cathedral was immense in the Spanish manner, with lots of space reserved for processions and hospitality towards itinerant pilgrims. The magnificent choir was enclosed. Judi fingered the elaborately carved walnut backs and arms of the stalls and wished she had had more time to explore the delights of Spain. *She didn't want to leave!* Her longing to stay was a physical pain, and she felt quite sick at the thought of never seeing Spain or Don Joaquin again.

They went next to the Sacristry containing El Greco's portraits of the Twelve Apostles. El Greco would give her something to hold on to, something to assuage the misery that was destroying her inch by inch as the afternoon wore on. The guide told them how the artist had visited the local madhouse to find his sitters for the portraits, and this explained the hopeless, patient look on their faces. Judi felt a strong sympathy for these tired, desperate people.

Once outside, they admired the cupola that had been designed by El Greco's son, and hurried on to the next point of interest. Judi's shoes actively hurt now. She would have liked to have taken them off for a few minutes, but she was afraid of getting lost if she paused, even for a moment, in the relentless pursuit of their guide.

Toledo had many memories of the Arab occupation. On the walnut choir-stalls it had been possible to see represented, one after another, the victories the Spaniards had inflicted on the Moors in their relentless, century-long reconquest of their land. Yet not all the Arabs had gone away. Many of them had been there so long they had nowhere else to go. The Arabs of Toledo had gone on living there just as they had before, leaving an indelible mark on Spanish architecture and customs.

The Jews also had made Toledo their home. In the middle ages, Toledo had been the Jerusalem of the Spanish Jews and many of the street names came straight from Palestine, pointing to the areas where they had lived before they, too, were chased out by an increasingly fanatical Inquisition.

The old synagogue of Santa Maria la Blanca is a combination of the genius of both Jews and Arabs. It was built for the Jews, but the first impression is that of an Arab-Andalusian mosque, with the well-learned lessons of the effects of light and space in a sun-drenched land. The synagogue had a sad history, for it became in turn a church, a home for repentant women, a barracks, a warehouse and now a museum.

Judi looked about her with pleasure, admiring the many columns and horseshoe arches that linked them together. The geometric adornments appealed to her professional eye, and she would have loved to have represented some of the designs in her own medium. If she were to live in Spain she would never lack for inspiration, she thought sadly. Everywhere she looked there was something to delight her eye and to add another strand binding her heart to a land and people that no longer seemed foreign to her.

It was sleeting outside. Judi turned up the collar of her coat, pausing to look up and down the lane where the synagogue was situated. A man stood at the top of the street, a man so like Don Joaquin that he took her breath away. She shut her eyes, praying he was a figment of her imagination, but when she opened them again he was still there, leaning against the wall, apparently oblivious of the slushy rain that was falling on his bare head.

His name burst from her lips. "Joaquin!" The man looked up and saw her in the same instant. Sheer panic made her take off down the street as fast as her high-heels would carry her, accompanied by cries from her fellow tourists and the repeated shouts of their guide.

"Come back! We go another way!"

Judi ran all the faster. She looked over her shoulder and saw that Joaquin had come up to the group and was questioning them, his charm very much in evidence. Her heart beat quicker at the sight. Ridiculous as it might be, she was *proud* of the way he looked and the way he spoke, bringing a glow to Carmen's face which hadn't been there earlier.

It didn't take long for Judi to realise she was hopelessly lost. She followed a sign that directed her to the new site of El Greco's most famous painting of all, *The Burial of the Count of Orgaz*. Her party would be bound to go there, she reasoned, and by that time they would have lost Don Joaquin and she would be safe.

She found her way more easily than she had expected. There was no one she knew outside the church where the painting was housed. She stepped cautiously inside, coming face to face with the enormous painting. She paused, lost in the stunning gold procession of saints who had come down to earth to welcome the Count into heaven.

"Where will you run to now, little Hudi?"

Judi started. "Oh, no!" she gasped.

"Did you think I'd lose you so easily?"

"I'm going back to England!"

Don Joaquin put a restraining hand on her shoulder. "I think not. Not until you've explained to me why you had to dash out of my home like a criminal, without a word of goodbye to anyone—"

"I said goodbye to Doña Maria. She quite understood—"

"Did she? Wasn't it to *me* that you owed some explanation? If she understands, I most certainly do not. I thought we'd agreed that you'd stay in Spain—"

"*You* decided I would! You never asked *me!*"

"Didn't I?" She recognised the flash in his eyes, renewing the urge to run while she could.

She took a step away from him. "You know you didn't."

"Perhaps I didn't think it necessary, not when it must be as obvious to you as it is to me that we are made for each other."

Her lips felt stiff and dry. "How did you know where I was?" she asked him.

"Fabiola saw you leave the castle and the proprietor of the *bodega* saw you getting on the bus. He was horrified to see you leaving with a suitcase in your hand just after he had been telling your group that our marriage had been announced and how glad the town was that I'd found a suitable wife at last."

"*Suitable?*" Judi stared at the painting with unseeing eyes. "In what way am I suitable?"

His hand felt warm and heavy on her shoulder. "Fabiola likes you."

"Everybody likes me!" she exclaimed.

"Except me," he said.

"Oh, I know that! You've already told me you don't like me at all! Though how you can want to marry someone you don't like is beyond me."

He bent his head until she could feel his breath on her cheek. "Shall I explain it to you?" he whispered.

She trembled at the ease with which he could stir her emotions. She longed to give way to the pressure of his hand and lean against him, abandoning forever her bid for freedom.

"I'm still going back to England!"

Her voice was trembling as much as she was. She cleared her throat and eased her feet in her uncomfortable shoes. The movement drew his attention to the cause of her distress.

"If you'd really been determined, you wouldn't have worn those shoes," he pointed out with a very masculine grin. He opened her coat, linking his hands together behind her back. "Come home with me, Hudi, and be mine."

She shook her head with a violence that tossed her hair out of shape. "My other shoes are packed!"

"You're trembling. Are you cold?"

His concern for her made her want to cry. She was cold, but she was even more fearful that she wouldn't have the strength of mind to go away from him again.

"A little," she said.

He straightened his back. "This isn't the place to have this sort of discussion. Will you trust yourself to my car?"

"Do I have any choice?"

He looked seriously into her storm-grey eyes. "I'll take you anywhere you want to go—after we've talked. We can go to a hotel, if you prefer, or to a café, or to my car, or—we could go home."

Judi swallowed nervously. "Not home! I don't want to see Leonor again. She—she—"

"How many times must I tell you that Leonor needn't concern you, *mi amor*?"

"I doubt she'd agree with you," Judi returned with a burst of spirit. "She hates me—"

"And Fabiola hates her. Does it matter, *querida*? Does it really matter?"

Judi lowered her eyes to the button of his coat, concentrating very hard on not allowing her tears to get the better of her. How very differently men and women looked at the world. No woman would ever consider housing her husband and her lover under one roof. Not unless she was the Empress of Russia, or similarly cushioned against the consequences of such awful folly. Did he really think that she and Leonor would become friends? Did he know so little about women that he couldn't see that Leonor would never be a friend to any other woman, and probably not to any man?

"It matters to me," she said.

The group she had been with came into the church in a scurry of booted feet and twirling umbrellas. The American woman saw Judi at once, a wide smile breaking over her face.

"We were afraid you got lost!" She looked at Don Joaquin with interest. "I see we needn't have worried. You are the fiancée after all, aren't you?"

"Yes," said Judi with a weary sigh.

Carmen followed close behind. She, too, looked relieved when she saw Judi, and she said something to Don Joaquin that Judi didn't catch. He answered in English with a cheerful laugh.

"My *novia* and I had a misunderstanding. It was my fault."

The two women dismissed that as so patently untrue that Judi could have strangled all three of them.

"All that matters to me is whether or not she is going on to Madrid with us," Carmen said to him, ignoring Judi as if she had not been there.

"I'm going with you!"

"She's coming with me."

They spoke together, but Carmen was only listening to Joaquin. "*Claro!*" she murmured, fluttering her eyelashes. She gathered her group together, the American included, and pressed forward to look at the painting. "*Qué lo pase bien!*" she added to Don Joaquin over her shoulder.

Enjoy himself indeed! What about her? Judi fumed. Didn't anyone in the world care what she thought about *anything*?

"I think we might do that, don't you?" Joaquin smiled at her, tilting his head to one side.

"No!" She flicked away a tear from her cheek. "Joaquin, I *want* to go with them! My luggage is on the coach and I'm not going back to the castle with only the clothes I have on. Moreover, I'm not going back to the castle at all!"

"We'll discuss it in the car after we get your luggage out of the bus," he told her calmly.

"You never give me any say in anything! You never *listen* to me!"

"*Niña*, I'll listen to you all night, but I'd rather not catch pneumonia while I'm doing it." His face softened dramatically as he saw her tears begin to fall in earnest. "Oh, *bombón*, what am I going to do with you?" he groaned.

At the familiar endearment her resolve broke and she threw herself into the circle of his arms.

"I didn't think you'd ever call me that again," she told him, her face buried in his coat.

His arms tightened about her. "How little you know me, my love," he said.

Chapter Eleven

Judi sat in the blessedly warm car watching the slushy rain fall all round her, melting as soon as it hit the ground. It was getting colder by the minute and she began to worry about Joaquin and what could be taking him so long. He had left his coat behind for her and she had wrapped it about herself like a blanket. Had the coach been parked so far away? Or perhaps the driver had refused to release her luggage to anyone but the owner.

She was wondering whether she should go after him when she saw him coming towards her. At the sight of him her heart melted, and she knew that come what may, she would never voluntarily go away from him again.

He threw her suitcase onto the back seat and himself onto the seat behind the wheel, slamming the door shut after him.

"Are you terribly cold?" she asked him.

Some flakes of snow had caught in his lashes and she wanted to brush them away, but the frozen look on his face made her change her mind.

"Do you care?"

The hopelessness in the words jolted her into looking at him again. "Of course I care!"

His lips twisted into a ghost of a smile. "So much that you'll take any opportunity to run away from me?"

She pushed a little of his coat towards him. "I wasn't running away from you," she said shakily.

He raised a brow. "No?"

She shook her head violently. "It was an impossible situation. You must see that! It wasn't fair to Leonor—or to me!"

"Then why the flood of tears when I caught up with you?"

A warmth crept up into her cheeks. "I was steeling myself to get used to the idea that I'd never see you again, and then, there you were. It was—it was reaction."

He turned towards her, putting an arm about her shoulders. "*Bombón*, you'll have to explain it to me better than that. I thought we'd come to an understanding. What went wrong?"

She moulded her body more comfortably against his, the first stirrings of desire rising within her as she felt the warmth of his body. How could she even have contemplated giving up all this? she wondered. She belonged to him, and she had for a long time now.

"Leonor—" she said.

His caress was impatient, rubbing a finger

down the side of her face and across her lips. "How many times must I tell you that Leonor has nothing to do with you?"

"She's a difficult person to ignore," Judi said dryly.

He was looking less cold and distant now as she kissed his finger in passing. "She is indeed! She's decided to go and stay with Pilar for awhile before going home to her parents. That lady outstayed her welcome some time ago!"

Judi's eyes became simply enormous, the smudged remains of her tears adding to her waiflike appearance. "Doesn't she want to marry you after all?"

"There was never any chance of Leonor becoming my wife."

Judi digested that in silence for a long moment. "Does your mother know?"

His smile was wry. "My mother finds Fabiola a bit much for her. Naturally, she wanted to see me married again. Was it she who told you I was going to marry Leonor?"

Judi nodded. "Such a *suitable* wife for you."

"That's all my mother knows! My first wife was suitable in every way but the one which matters most. I won't make that mistake a second time!"

Judi began to feel distinctly better. She managed a shy smile. "I shouldn't have thought Leonor is lacking in fire and passion."

"No," he mused. "Shows what an innocent you are, my love. A man wants to mean more to his wife than a looking glass for her to admire her own reflection in."

"Oh," said Judi.

"Yes, 'oh,' my sweet. Leonor fancies living in a

castle, but she didn't want to marry *me* any more than her cousin had. Neither duty nor ambition will warm a man's bed."

"Oh," Judi said again, a little embarrassed by his frankness.

His face was very close to hers. "Perhaps I wasn't very fair to you, *favorita*, but I had to be very sure this time. Is it too much to ask that my wife should love me for myself alone?"

She shook her head, her emotions in a whirl. "I love you, Joaquin," she said under her breath.

"Enough to have me make love to you before we go back to the castle?"

She nodded again, feeling shyer than ever. His eyes held hers, and the glint in them cut her to the quick. "Are you sure?"

"Yes, I'm quite sure." It was only a ribbon of sound and she wondered if he would hear her, but she could no more have repeated herself than fly.

She made no move to stop him, holding her breath as he pushed back the material of her dress, burying his face in the valley between her breasts and kissing the small hollow at the base of her neck.

He sat up with sudden decision, pulling her dress back together.

"This is too public a place. I'll drive to a place I know where there won't be anyone to disturb us."

She sat quietly, the colour hot in her cheeks while he watched her.

"What? No comment?"

She shook her head.

"Strange," he went on. "I never thought you

would let any man have you without a ring on your finger."

"I didn't think so either!" she said with a gasp.

He bent over her again, his lips tantalising hers until they opened to admit his tongue. His mouth was hard and demanding against hers, his hands on either side of her face to hold her still.

"I want you so badly!" he whispered at last, reluctantly releasing her. "I want all your love, and your body, and the sweet, sweet womanly essence of you. Do you want me?"

"*Yes!*" she burst out.

He kissed her one last time, running his tongue round her lips. "Good," he said. He tucked his coat in round her and smiled into her solemn, grey eyes. "You can never want me too much, *bombón*. Remember that."

How could she forget? The sweet torment he had aroused in her tore at her entrails, longing for him to fulfil her need for him. Was it always like this with the man one loved, she wondered. Would she always feel this painful urgency in her blood that fed on the sight and touch of him until it threatened to overwhelm her altogether, sweeping her into a never-ending vortex of desire?

Joaquin set the car in motion, negotiating the narrow streets with all the confidence of one who came to Toledo frequently and knew it well. Judi watched his hands on the wheel and her flesh prickled as she remembered the feel of them against her breasts. She wrenched her eyes away and looked out of the window with determination.

"Doña Maria will never forgive you if you don't marry," she said out loud.

He shrugged his shoulders. "My mother doesn't rule my life. No woman does."

"Didn't Teresa?"

A muscle jerked in his cheek. "Are you jealous of a dead woman, Hudi?"

"No."

But she wasn't sure that that was the truth. She was jealous of any and every woman who had ever known him. She wanted him to be as much hers as she was his.

"Not even of Leonor?"

Her hands clenched into two fists. "Leonor is—unhappy—" she began uncertainly.

"I wonder. She always throws a tantrum if she can't get her own way. I hope Fabiola doesn't go the same way."

Judi was shocked. "But Fabiola's *your* daughter."

He glanced at her, his expression full of self-mockery. "I've quite a temper myself when roused, as you might have experienced this afternoon if you hadn't threatened to drown me in tears before I got started.

Judi sat up very straight. "I don't believe you."

"Take it as a warning," he advised her, and she couldn't be certain whether he was serious or not, "and don't ever try to run out on me again."

She threaded her fingers together, seeking the words that would explain her motives to him, motives that she was beginning to wonder if she fully understood herself.

"I thought you'd be glad to find me gone! That

you'd been as embarrassed by Fabiola's announcement as I was."

His lopsided smile set her heart knocking against her ribs. "Weren't you embarrassed?" she asked, somewhat timidly.

"No."

"Well everyone else was! Your mother didn't know where to look! And I—I was devastated—"

"You looked it!"

"—on Leonor's behalf," Judi finished with dignity. "It was a cruel thing to do to her."

Joaquin put his hand on hers, brushing against her thigh and making her muscles flex with unexpected delight.

"Forget Leonor, *bombón*. She knew I was never going to marry her."

"But Joaquin, she didn't!"

His eyes narrowed as he stared at the road ahead of them. "How do you know, Hudi?"

"She was furious! She hates me, and I've never been hated before. She—she wouldn't have behaved like that if she hadn't thought you—you were fond of her, at least."

"What did she do?"

Judi was silent. If he didn't know, she wasn't going to be the one to tell him. Leonor had been humiliated enough by being sent away from the castle—for that's how she would regard her stay with Pilar, Judi was sure of that—without exposing her to anything more, no matter how well-deserved.

"It was I who sent the announcements to the papers," Joaquin said abruptly.

"*You*? But why? You don't want to marry me!"

"Don't I? What do you think I'm going to do with you?"

"I don't know!"

He drove a short way off the road onto the crown of a deserted hill. A whole valley, empty except for some browsing animals, stretched out before them. There was not a single house to be seen anywhere, nor any other human being. They could have been completely alone in the world.

For a long moment he kept his hands on the wheel, looking straight ahead, and so deep was his concentration on his own thoughts that Judi began to wonder if he had forgotten all about her.

When he spoke his voice was carefully neutral, but she could feel, even if she couldn't hear, the edge of anger in it.

"Tell me, Hudi, if I'm not going to marry you, what am I going to do with you?"

"I—I thought—"

"God save us from women who think!"

Judi was indignant. "Well, how was I to know?" she demanded. "You never said you wanted to marry me. Never mind that it never occurred to you to ask me. As far as I knew it was all arranged for you to marry Leonor."

"And keep you as my mistress?" His hands shone white on the wheel. "No wonder you ran away from me."

"But I didn't. Never from you! I'd have stayed if there had only been you to consider, but I couldn't take what didn't belong to me, not even from Leonor. I couldn't."

"Leonor," he said bitterly. "We always come back to Leonor! Who told you I was going to marry her? Or did you invent the idea for yourself?"

"It was well known," she hedged, flinching away from the purposeful gleam in his eyes. "Your mother told me," she conceded. "She told me the day I arrived with you from Avila."

"I seem to remember telling you at some length what I wanted from a wife. Did it sound like a portrait of Leonor?"

"Yes," she said, "I thought it did."

"But you don't even like her!"

"No," Judi admitted carefully. "I'm not a man though. I was trying to see her through your eyes."

He covered his face with his hands. "Oh dear, I did make a mess of it, didn't I? I thought I was trying to reassure you that it was quite all right for you to feel as you do about me, that I *welcomed* it, especially coming from you. I didn't want you to think I'd reject you as your ex-fiancé did—that I'd fall for someone else as soon as you turned your back."

A gleam of sunlight broke through the leaden skies, lighting up the valley and bathing it in a yellow evening light. Judi saw it like the echo of her own spirits. Joaquin had cared for her much more than she had imagined and she swiftly sought to comfort him.

"You did tell me," she confessed, "only my head was full of what your mother had said about your having to make a suitable marriage. I hated that word *suitable!* You said you'd made one marriage to suit your family, that the next one would be to suit yourself, but I never, in my wildest dreams, thought you'd look in my direction. My family lives in a cottage, not a castle."

He moved towards her, his eyes on her mouth. "I knew just how *suitable* you were, my darling, the first time I kissed you. The second time, I would have taken you to bed then and there, but you looked so lost and bewildered I thought you needed time to get used to the idea. I told myself that when the time came, you wouldn't be able to resist me."

Judi blushed, thinking how true that was. "No wonder you looked so smug," she said.

"I'd discovered how sweet you are, *bombón*. I had something to be smug about."

She put up a hand, tracing his strong mouth with a finger. "I discovered something, too. When I became engaged to David I thought I was very much in love with him, but I never felt for him what I feel for you."

"I know that."

She bridled. "How can you know?"

"Because you wouldn't have allowed him to make love to you without a ring on your finger."

His lips gently touched hers, coaxing her into forgetting her dismay that he should be able to read her heart so exactly while his still remained a closed book to her. His hand reached for her zipper a second time and she arched against him to make it easier for him.

"You are going to let me make love to you, aren't you?" he breathed against her throat.

"Yes."

"You don't want to wait until we're married?"

She shook her head, her mouth finding his with an urgency that reverberated through her body. "I love you, Joaquin. I love you more than life itself."

Her own hands were as busy as his, unbuttoning his shirt and exploring the hair-roughened skin of his chest, rejoicing in his strongly muscled shoulders and back. There was no other man in the world who could make her feel this way. She thought with a moment of regret that she wasn't his wife when he first made love to her, so what did it matter that he couldn't wait? She was his whenever he chose to take her.

There was a rhythm in his kisses which aroused her to a peak of desire, and she became more daring still, exploring his body with the same freedom that he was exploring hers. Her breasts ached for his touch and she groaned with relief when his fingers and then his mouth, found her nipples, before returning to her lips in a kiss more wildly satisfying than any which had gone before.

She was at a loss when he drew back from her, searching his face to see how she could have failed him.

"What's the matter?" she asked in a shaky voice.

"*Es la primera vez*?" he said in Spanish. It was more a statement than a question.

"You know it is," she answered him, puzzled. "Don't you want me after all?"

"Do I want you? Dear Heaven, how I want you!"

He sounded furiously angry. "I was trying to prove something to myself. My love, I thought I could make love to you, casually, in a car, and that you wouldn't be able to refuse me, that I'd know then that you were mine to love whenever I wanted to. But I can't do it to you. You deserve a better time and place than this. I'll take you to bed when I have the blessing of the Church and State, and not before! It's the only way I can begin to prove to you how much I love you."

"You love me?" The wonder of it shone in her eyes. "Oh, Joaquin, are you sure? You don't just want to make love to me?"

"I did," he admitted. "I didn't want to love a woman ever again, but I can't help loving you. This time, I told myself, it was all going to be different. I vowed I'd never beg a woman for anything again, but take it from her as my right. But I can't do that to you, my love. I want everything to be perfect for you, no matter what it costs me in frustration. Come to my arms and let me kiss you again!"

Spanish was the language of love, she thought as soon as she could think at all. It sounded as smooth as butter to her ears, even though much of it she couldn't understand, as it had been outside the scope of any lessons she had received at evening classes. But what did it matter? It all came down to the same thing. She loved Joaquin and, joy of joys, he loved her, too! With time and patience, she would show him that, unlike Teresa, she was more than prepared to welcome the consequences of that love, that she was as eager for his passion as she had been reluctant.

She laughed out loud, impatient to take up the new life he was offering her, burying her fingers deep in his hair and pulling his head down to hers.

"It's turned out to be a lovely evening. Joaquin, if you're not going to make love to me now, let's go home and tell Fabiola and your mother. I ought to telephone my parents, too."

He groaned softly, biting the lobe of her ear. "Let us go! But don't take too long about it, *bombón, mi amor,* because I'm not waiting more than a couple of weeks for you! Is it understood?"

She touched his lashes with her fingertips, her lips curling into a smile. "I'll always be there whenever you want me," she promised. "You have only to call and I'll come."

Her parents came before the wedding, making much of Fabiola, and fitting in with the life of the castle with a calm that made Judi proud of them. Her mother volunteered to help her with her wedding dress, but it was the nuns who insisted on doing all the final touches, working day and night to get it ready for her in time.

Padre Juan was afraid she would want to make her vows in English, but Judi preferred to speak to Joaquin in his own language when she put her future unreservedly into his hands. She wanted there to be no doubt in his mind that her commitment was full and final, that he was all she wanted from life.

Pilar came to the wedding, but not Leonor. Pilar was accompanied by her husband and two boys, both of whom did everything to console Fabiola for being away from her father and Judi for a time. Pilar, as charming and as sensible as ever, also made arrangements to take Judi's parents to the airport after the ceremony, thus freeing Judi from the last worry she had before she found herself alone in the castle with her new husband. Even Doña Maria and Padre Juan had gone on a visit to another branch of the family.

"Men have all the fun!" Fabiola had complained to Judi the night before the wedding.

"Do they?" Judi had tried not to laugh.

"What fun do girls have?"

"I wouldn't be marrying your father if I wasn't a girl," Judi had pointed out. "And as I want to do that more than anything else in the world, why should I want to be a man?"

Fabiola had kissed her with quick affection. *"Es muy hombre mi Papa!"* she acknowledged frankly. "When I'm grown up, my husband will be the same!"

Judi remembered those words as she sat in Joaquin's room, waiting for her husband. His quarters were in the twin tower to where she had slept all this time, having much the same view. Judi had stood by the window for the first few moments before she had begun to undress in a panic. Now she was trying to calm herself by sitting on the stool in front of the dressing-table, brushing her hair until it shone.

Tonight would be a test for both of them, she thought. Any reluctance on her part and he would wonder if she would be as cold towards him as Teresa had been, yet she was bound to be nervous this first time, not knowing exactly what was in store for her, even though she wanted to be with Joaquin as much as she had ever wanted anything.

He came to her through the bathroom, his hair wet from his shower and with only his silk dressing gown to cover him. Judi's eyes were drawn towards him despite the deepening pink in her cheeks, and she drew the edges of her own gown about her more tightly.

He came and stood behind her, looking deep into her shadowed eyes in the mirror. "You looked beautiful today," he said. "The bride of my dreams."

She smiled, her nervousness gone for the moment. "You looked *muy hombre*, as Fabiola is always pointing out," she returned the compliment.

He raised his eyebrows. "Hadn't you noticed for yourself?" he teased her gently.

She nodded, as shy of him as she had been before. She put down her hairbrush and turned to face him.

"You don't have to be Spanish to notice these things," she murmured. "Right back, in Avila—"

He put his hands on her shoulders and arched her backwards. "My dear love, fascinating as these reminiscences are, I have waited for you quite long enough. Come to bed!"

She reached for his kiss and then stood up, letting her negligée swing out behind her. She ran her hands down the lace it was made of, swaying slightly where she stood. Should she take it off?

It was he who pushed it back from her shoulders and down her arms, letting it fall to the ground at her feet. Her nightdress followed with a despatch that made her gasp, but she refused to turn away from the look in his eyes. This was the moment she had been waiting for, and she refused to give way to the quivering nervousness that had settled somewhere in her middle and was making war with the desire that rose inevitably to his touch.

His hands were on her shoulders and then on her breasts, sliding down to her waist, and then to her hips, holding her close against the hardening of his own need for her. He swung her off her feet and laid her down on the bed, shedding his own covering as he joined her, sliding his naked body down beside hers.

Her nervousness died as his arms went about her. There was nothing left but her need to please him and to please herself by doing so.

"I'll try not to hurt you, *bombón*," he whispered against her mouth. "If I do, it'll be the only time I will."

She was more than ready for him, however, when the moment came and their joint passion reached an unbearable turbulence before surging into a shared exultation she would never forget.

The sun was making its first appearance over the horizon when she slipped from the bed to tidy the room of the clothes they had dropped where they stood. She felt very much the wife as she picked up his silk gown and placed it at the foot of the bed. Her husband was still sleeping and it was a perfect opportunity to study him at his most vulnerable.

He woke immediately, watching her through narrowed eyes. "Well, beloved," he asked her, "was it as perfect for you as it was for me?"

She bent over and kissed him full on the mouth. "Perhaps even more perfect," she whispered, before he reached for her again.

6 brand new
Silhouette Special Editions
yours for 15 days–Free!

For the reader who wants more…more story…more detail and description…more realism…and more romance…in paperback originals, 1/3 longer than our regular Silhouette Romances. Love lingers longer in new Silhouette Special Editions. Love weaves an intricate, provocative path in a third more pages than you have just enjoyed. It is love as you have always wanted it to be—and more —intriguingly depicted by your favorite Silhouette authors in the inimitable Silhouette style.

15-Day Free Trial Offer

We will send you 6 new Silhouette Special Editions to keep for 15 days absolutely free! If you decide not to keep them, send them back to us, you pay nothing. But if you enjoy them as much as we think you will, keep them and pay the invoice enclosed with your trial shipment. You will then automatically become a member of the Special Edition Book Club and receive 6 more romances every month. There is no minimum number of books to buy and you can cancel at any time.

── FREE CHARTER MEMBERSHIP COUPON ──

Silhouette Special Editions, Dept. SESB-1G
120 Brighton Road, Clifton, NJ 07012

Please send me 6 Silhouette Special Editions to keep for 15 days, absolutely free. I understand I am not obligated to join the Silhouette Special Editions Book Club unless I decide to keep them.

Name _____

Address _____

City _____

State _____ Zip _____

This offer expires January 31, 1983

Silhouette Romance

IT'S YOUR OWN SPECIAL TIME

Contemporary romances for today's women.
Each month, six very special love stories will be yours
from SILHOUETTE. Look for them wherever books are sold
or order now from the coupon below.

$1.50 each

Hampson	☐ 1 ☐ 4 ☐ 16 ☐ 27 ☐ 28 ☐ 52 ☐ 94	Browning	☐ 12 ☐ 38 ☐ 53 ☐ 73 ☐ 93
Stanford	☐ 6 ☐ 25 ☐ 35 ☐ 46 ☐ 58 ☐ 88	Michaels	☐ 15 ☐ 32 ☐ 61 ☐ 87
		John	☐ 17 ☐ 34 ☐ 57 ☐ 85
Hastings	☐ 13 ☐ 26	Beckman	☐ 8 ☐ 37 ☐ 54 ☐ 96
Vitek	☐ 33 ☐ 47 ☐ 84	Wisdom	☐ 49 ☐ 95
Wildman	☐ 29 ☐ 48	Halston	☐ 62 ☐ 83

☐ 5 Goforth	☐ 22 Stephens	☐ 50 Scott	☐ 81 Roberts
☐ 7 Lewis	☐ 23 Edwards	☐ 55 Ladame	☐ 82 Dailey
☐ 9 Wilson	☐ 24 Healy	☐ 56 Trent	☐ 86 Adams
☐ 10 Caine	☐ 30 Dixon	☐ 59 Vernon	☐ 89 James
☐ 11 Vernon	☐ 31 Halldorson	☐ 60 Hill	☐ 90 Major
☐ 14 Oliver	☐ 36 McKay	☐ 63 Brent	☐ 92 McKay
☐ 19 Thornton	☐ 39 Sinclair	☐ 71 Ripy	☐ 97 Clay
☐ 20 Fulford	☐ 43 Robb	☐ 76 Hardy	☐ 98 St. George
☐ 21 Richards	☐ 45 Carroll	☐ 78 Oliver	☐ 99 Camp

$1.75 each

Stanford	☐ 100 ☐ 112 ☐ 131	Hampson	☐ 108 ☐ 119 ☐ 128 ☐ 136 ☐ 147 ☐ 151 ☐ 155
Hardy	☐ 101 ☐ 130	Browning	☐ 113 ☐ 142
Cork	☐ 103 ☐ 148	Michaels	☐ 114 ☐ 146
Vitek	☐ 104 ☐ 139 ☐ 157	Beckman	☐ 124 ☐ 154
Dailey	☐ 106 ☐ 118 ☐ 153	Roberts	☐ 127 ☐ 143
Bright	☐ 107 ☐ 125		

$1.75 each

☐ 102 Hastings	☐ 120 Carroll	☐ 133 Rowe	☐ 145 Hope
☐ 105 Eden	☐ 121 Langan	☐ 134 Charles	☐ 149 Saunders
☐ 109 Vernon	☐ 122 Scofield	☐ 135 Logan	☐ 150 Major
☐ 110 Trent	☐ 123 Sinclair	☐ 137 Hunter	☐ 152 Halston
☐ 111 South	☐ 126 St. George	☐ 138 Wilson	☐ 156 Sawyer
☐ 115 John	☐ 129 Converse	☐ 140 Erskine	☐ 158 Reynolds
☐ 116 Lindley	☐ 132 Wisdom	☐ 144 Goforth	☐ 159 Tracy
☐ 117 Scott			

___ # 160 STRANGERS MAY MARRY Hampson   ___ # 166 DREAMS FROM THE PAST Wisdom
___ # 161 RUN FROM HEARTACHE Trent   ___ # 167 A SILVER NUTMEG Hunter
___ # 162 ONE MAN FOREVER Ashby   ___ # 168 MOONLIGHT AND MEMORIES Carr
___ # 163 SEARCH FOR LOVE Roberts   ___ # 169 LOVER COME BACK Scott
___ # 164 ISLAND ON THE HILL Browning   ___ # 170 A TREASURE OF LOVE Ripy
___ # 165 ARRANGED MARRIAGE Young   ___ # 171 LADY MOON Hill

LOOK FOR *MERMAID'S TOUCH* BY PATTI BECKMAN
AVAILABLE IN OCTOBER AND
DARK FANTASY BY LAURA HARDY
IN NOVEMBER.

- - - - - - - - - - - - - - - - -

SILHOUETTE BOOKS, Department SB/1
1230 Avenue of the Americas
New York, NY 10020

Please send me the books I have checked above. I am enclosing
$_____ (please add 50¢ to cover postage and handling. NYS and
NYC residents please add appropriate sales tax). Send check or
money order—no cash or C.O.D.'s please. Allow six weeks for delivery.

NAME_____

ADDRESS_____

CITY_____STATE/ZIP_____

Silhouette Desire
15-Day Trial Offer
A new romance series that explores contemporary relationships in exciting detail

Four Silhouette Desire romances, free for 15 days!
We'll send you four new Silhouette Desire romances to look over for 15 days, absolutely free! If you decide not to keep the books, return them and owe nothing.

Four books a month, free home delivery. If you like Silhouette Desire romances as much as we think you will, keep them and return your payment with the invoice. Then we will send you four new books every month to preview, just as soon as they are published. You pay only for the books you decide to keep, and you never pay postage and handling.

------ MAIL TODAY ------

Silhouette Desire, Dept. SDSR 7H
120 Brighton Road, Clifton, NJ 07012

Please send me 4 Silhouette Desire romances to keep for 15 days, absolutely free. I understand I am not obligated to join the Silhouette Desire Book Club unless I decide to keep them.

Name_____

Address_____

City_____

State_____ Zip_____

This offer expires March 31, 1983

Silhouette Romance

Coming next month from
Silhouette Romances

Logic Of The Heart by Dixie Browning

Emma was looking forward to seeing the romantic island of Hatteras, and meeting Dan Slater added to the magic. She could see herself slipping into his arms and falling under his spell. . . .

Devil's Bargain by Elaine Camp

Was Alexis being caught up in an evil scheme or was Drayce's renewed love for her genuine? Their once passionate marriage seemed too distant to recapture those lost moments of ecstasy. Yet suddenly Drayce made Alexis forget why escape was so important!

Flight To Romance by Tracy Sinclair

Jennifer was not going to refuse Kalim Al Kahira, when he asked her to return with him to Egypt. She told herself her career demanded that she go—until she realized that there was no way to refuse his dark, penetrating eyes.

In Name Only by Roxanne Jarrett

Jill traveled to Brazil to enter into an arranged marriage. She was determined not to be ruled by her new husband, but soon she found herself unable to deny the mad passions that filled her with desire.

Sweet Surrender by Donna Vitek

Suzanne's trip to Italy turned out to be anything but the quiet visit she anticipated. For once she met Jared Caine she felt compelled to compete for his attention and show him the depth and breadth of her love.

The Second Time by Janet Dailey

Dawn returned home to the Florida Keys to seek peace in the turquoise waters. But soon calm waters are turned into turbulent seas when passions are ignited by her old flame Slater MacBride.

Genuine Silhouette sterling silver bookmark for only $15.95!

What a beautiful way to hold your place in your current romance! This genuine sterling silver bookmark, with the distinctive Silhouette symbol in elegant black, measures 1½″ long and 1″ wide. It makes a beautiful gift for yourself, and for every romantic you know! And, at only $15.95 each, including all postage and handling charges, you'll want to order several now, while supplies last.

Send your name and address with check or money order for $15.95 per bookmark ordered to

Simon & Schuster Enterprises
120 Brighton Rd., P.O. Box 5020
Clifton, N.J. 07012
Attn: Bookmark

Bookmarks can be ordered pre-paid only. No charges will be accepted. Please allow 4-6 weeks for delivery.

N.Y. State Residents
Please Add Sales Tax